Prosecution.

A NOVEL

Richard Chandler

Second Edition

Layout by Rachel Greene for elfinpen designs.

Cover Design by Ms. Amelia S. Greene for Penoaks Publishing.

ISBN: 979-8-84741-520-0

One.

Ojo Teferra began work on his first murder case on July 1st, only two days after the funeral of his father-in-law. The summer heat had increased steadily since the early June rains, unseasonable and unexpected, the high humidity turning even the occasional breezes uncomfortable, so much so it made the lead story on the local news that morning.

The Ministry of Justice building for Shewa Province was among the most ornate in downtown

Addis Ababa, Ethiopia's capital city—it dated from 1970, and while not the tallest in among more modern skyscrapers and business centers, it distinguished itself with its beautiful architecture, and its grounds, and its concentric rectangles of eucalyptus trees and small statues. Even the usually temperate Addis Ababa was far too warm, summer arriving with a vengeance, and locals coping as best they could with extreme weather that proved unrelenting til well after sundown.

When Ojo arrived on that Monday morning the Ministry was already busy with a flood of local cases; he wound his way through the crowded lobby to a crowded elevator, then to his third floor office, to quickly prepare for his impending meeting with the justice minister. He had already prepared a paper folder on the Mgbato case, but now needed to update online as to fresh developments. He did not want any surprises to pop up in this most important meeting regarding his first murder case.

Ojo had lived in Addis Ababa nearly all his life, having moved from his parents' home shortly after graduating public school; his middle-class parents had just the one son, so he never wanted for attention. They also had sky-high hopes for their young man who was cleverer and more observant from an early age—his keen mind served him well at university, and his inquisitive and imaginative turn suggested a future in academics, science or law; Ojo chose law, perhaps for its innate stability, and perhaps in part because he himself disliked disorder whether in mind, personal habit or society.

Chaos was to be feared, especially when one considered the social and political history of his native Ethiopia; and so skilled was Ojo as a barrister, that he rose to a kind of prominence in his profession before turning forty, and forty being his current age.

Justice Minister Zenawi's offices occupied one fifth of the third floor, with an anteroom nearly the size of Ojo's entire office—his secretary congratulated Ojo on having been assigned such a high-profile homicide so early in his career, as Ojo had been with for only five years; but then he also knew, not much was at stake overall for the Ministry, as the case was unlikely to reverberate politically, and continued unrest in neighboring Eritrea to the north would likely occupy media interest all through the summer.

After just a few minutes, Ojo was escorted into Zenawi's spacious and richly-decorated office.

"Good morning, Ojo," Uba Zenawi said, and shook his hand. "I am sorry to have kept you waiting at all, but I was on a call from *Addis Abmas*—there is considerable press interest in this case, as you can appreciate."

"Very good morning, Uba," said Ojo, and took the chair opposite. "And yes, I do appreciate the gravity involved." This conversation was of course spoken in Amharic, the dominant language in Ethiopia.

"On such warm days as these, I find myself grateful for these light-fabric suits," Zenawi mentioned as he sat.

"It's expected to hit nearly 100."

"You know, some people think I turned down a judgeship for political reasons—the truth is, I just didn't want to have to wear black in the summer." He smiled at his own jest, then turned more serious. "I understand your family buried your wife's father this weekend, I am sorry—did you know him well?"

"Thank you…no, I didn't know him well; he and Afia were not as close as they had once been, even though he lived not far from us."

He nodded. "How is she doing?"

"She's very strong," Ojo said with some pride. "Afia has handled it very well—perhaps because Kashka had been in poor health for some time. This was not sudden, as it had been with the loss of her mother."

"I understand," he replied. "Next year I turn sixty, and I still have both parents, thank the heavens…please convey my sympathies."

"Thank you, sir."

He consulted his terminal. "I do want to discuss the Mgbako case with you, Ojo—but I also need to tell you, you'll have a new deputy prosecutor to assist you as second chair."

This surprised him. "What happened to Kitame?"

"He's reassigned to Environmental Affairs," Zenawi said. "Your new deputy will be Janan Takelo- she's a third-year prosecutor, top of her class, two years in Felony Fraud; she's a first-rate legal analyst, Ojo; and very pretty, which may work to your advantage in trial."

"That's a dubious strategy," Ojo said.

"Is it? Many studies have shown that attractive people prove more persuasive with the general public, fairly or not—just look at popular advertisements."

He smiled. "So, if we don't win our case, we can compensate by selling something."

"It would offset the trial costs," Zenawi grinned, and motioned to Janan's folder. "Is that the preliminary file on Mgbato?"

Ojo shared the folder. "The case seems straightforward—the victim was Nega Alemu, the tribal healer for the Tahaku tribe; he had promised the defendant's mother that his traditional remedies could cure her cancer; when she died of the disease, the defendant murdered Alemu out of revenge."

"Can we prove premeditation?"

"Alemu was stabbed with a small, straight blade—probably a typical kitchen knife; police have yet to discover the murder weapon."

"An average kitchen knife would be easy to conceal, and easily disposed of."

Ojo nodded. "Just so, unfortunately."

"If not, he confronted Alemu, lost his temper, and stabbed him in the heat of the moment with a knife conveniently at hand…there are no witnesses?"

There were not. "But Ngbato cannot establish an alibi, either—he says home, alone, the afternoon of the killing."

"That he didn't construct an alibi could argue his innocence; at least, a jury might think so."

"He confronted Alemu two days prior," Ojo mentioned. "He threatened him."

"Two days prior," Zenawi echoed. "What about his behavior when the police questioned him?"

"He was upset, nervous—he was acting suspiciously, nor could he deny that he and Alemu had words, as there were witnesses to their confrontation."

He paused. "The police say he was acting like a guilty man." Ojo confirmed this. "maybe, because he knew he had to be suspected of the crime? Ngbato is only nineteen—might it bring more suspicion on him, if he reacted in a more collected manner?"

"I cannot say, I didn't kill anyone when I was nineteen.'

"Well at last, that's on the record." He returned the folder to Ojo. "I've assigned Ms. Kelbessa the office adjacent yours—go meet her, get to know her, discuss the case. The pretrial set for the 16th, so you have two weeks to see eye to eye as to strategy in regards to both the case, and handling of the media. Good luck."

Janan Takelo was still moving her office items in when Ojo knocked at her open door. "I'm Ojo Teferra, District Junior Prosecutor," he announced. "We'll be working the case together."

"Janan Takelo—I'm pleased to meet you." She was indeed a very pretty young woman, not so tall, but with lovely smooth skin and long straight hair, but it was her big shining eyes and long straight nose that gained her the most attention. "We have met before, at the retirement party for Justice Nahom; you were handling an embezzlement case at that time."

Ojo was impressed—Okal Nahom's retirement party was over three years prior. He asked if he could pitch in, and began handing her file folders. "We have pretrial motions on the 10th, so we'll need to hit the ground running."

"I'll be scheduling interviews with friends and potential witnesses tomorrow afternoon," Janan said with a smile. "Today I'll be meeting with the investigating officers."

"Very good," he replied. "Have you accessed depositions on the case?"

She glanced to her computer, then to his folder. "I created a file once I was assigned—is this your way of implying that you're old school?"

"I find the heft reassuring," Ojo said.

She leaned against her desk. "As I understand it, this is your first homicide prosecution?" She confirmed this. "It's mine, as well—don't you find that odd, that we're assigned such a high-profile case?"

"When we might have caught some liquor-store shooting?" He leaned beside her in a similar way. "Do you think the Ministry is showing a reckless confidence in us?"

Janan hesitated. "Do you think there might be an ulterior motive?"

He sighed. "For now, let's you and I concentrate on Ngbato's motive, and whether it presents a problem."

"Ngbato's mother dies on May 21th, Ngbato confronts Alemu on the 22nd—the murder occurs on the 24th…" She pushed off, and placed a box of knickknacks on her desk. "The overarching question will be whether the crime might have been premeditated."

"And, if the knife belonged to Alemu?"

She shrugged. "Then it could have been spontaneous; or, he went to Alemu's home intending to kill him, and used a weapon of convenience—less compelling."

"Not necessarily, though we might have to explain why Alemu left a kitchen knife laying around."

"He was cooking?"

"That afternoon, we all were," he remarked. "I'm told the police are still actively looking for the weapon, so they're apparently confident it could be found?"

"Arresting officers arrived at Ngbato's home inside half an hour," Janan said. "That seems remarkably fast to me."

"Especially since there were no witnesses," Ojo said. "Ask about it when you meet the investigating officers tomorrow. We need to establish a timeline; if it raises more questions, we need to address them before trial."

Janan finally sat behind her new desk. "What will you be doing?"

"I'll be reviewing witness statements." He then placed the last moving box on her desk. "then I'll schedule a meeting with Ngbato's attorney, so we can prepare our own pretrial motions."

She brought a framed picture from the other box, of herself and an older woman posing before *Tis Isat*, the Blue Nile Falls. "This is my mother, Kafi; she's the one who encouraged me to go into law."

"She looks just like you," Ojo said.

"I've heard that you're married to a model, is that true?"

He smiled. "An ex-model—Afia now works in Municipal Archives... she didn't model for long, and she certainly wasn't famous."

"She was lucky, then," Janan said, which caught his attention, his curiosity all the keener when she didn't elucidate. "Still, I will bet that you have a copy of every single magazine that featured her, tucked away somewhere at home."

"I did have several of them, but she gave them away," he told her. "Afia almost never mentions her modeling...her traveling, yes; but, not the work itself."

"Work?" Janan gave a look. "You pose, you wait—they shoot; and for that, you make a fortune. Models will tell you the hours are long and the photographers exasperating, but really, how bad can it be?"

"In Afia's case I never asked."

That caught her attention. "Really?"

"She modeled only one season more after we met, and she is a private person."

"Evidently," Janan said; this could have been descriptive, or critical.

Ojo changed topics abruptly. "If the press corner you about this case, tell them it's ongoing, developing, evolving, all that line—but watch yourself, they can be relentless in coming down on you."

"That's why they're called the press," she said.

Ojo arrived home just after 6pm; he had left the Ministry at five, but traffic in the downtown of Addis Ababa is horrendous, overcrowded, and snarly, and no-one can drive any distance quickly during the rush hours; moreover, not only are the locals infamous for being poor drivers, but the recent heatwave sent tempers flaring, and aggravated that much more by the inevitable traffic jams.

Afia didn't face so long a drive home, and so was cushy and comfy for some while before Ojo made it home—it was like this every weekday, and she sometimes lorded it over him, though this night she wisely chose not to. "I've prepared some injera with chicken," she told him once he was in, "and the ice tea should be quite cold by now. Did you stop on the way?"

"No; that's how bad the traffic was tonight, it takes less than half that drive to drive in." They briefly kissed, and he hung up his suit jacket. "Have you been home long?"

"About thirty minutes—you took so long, I thought about taking a nap," she claimed, and she smiled. Afia Selassie was just beautiful—tall and slim, with shimmery hair, long limbs and a natural grace, she was all her adult life the center of attention; her dark eyes, high cheekbones and perfect teeth were the envy of most women who knew her. She had only recently turned thirty, and was not only seemingly ageless, but somehow timeless. "And I thought that, after dinner, we could go for a stroll."

"It's still over 90 out there," he warned, as he took off his tie.

"So it is," Afia teased.

Ojo and Afia lived in the Piazza, which included some of the best shopping and entertainment venues in Addis Ababa, including four new bookstores and two new theaters. The temperature was indeed still above 90 when they went for their walk, and unsurprisingly no-one else could be seen out. Both Ojo and were now dressed in lighter clothes, Afia in a pale loose blouse and a flimsy white skirt that showcased her long strong legs. "You said Bahiru is already in trouble in his new position," Ojo mentioned, referring to Afia's co-worker.

"Maybe, it's just as well you didn't win the promotion."

"That he's having trouble, doesn't mean I would," she asserted, referring to her mid-level position at the Municipal Archives, where she'd risen quickly in just a few years. "If Bahiru cannot manage it I'll still be there."

"It still surprises me that you find that position fulfilling."

"It's necessary work, it has to be done."

"There are others that can do necessary work."

"You're sounding elitist," Afia said. "There is nothing wrong with endless, mind-numbing paper-shuffling…I don't think I could do what you do, you play with peoples' futures."

"I assess peoples' past," Ojo minced, "and I help reveal the truth—worthwhile, I'd say."

"Open to interpretation." They strolled on, but it took only a few blocks before the heat became bothersome. "Today was your first day on the Mgbato case—any surprises?"

"Only that Kitame won't be my second chair," Ojo said. "My new assistant prosecutor is Janan Takelo, who's transferred from Theft and Robbery."

"So, you may want to count your pencils each day," Afia said with a grin.

Two.

Addis Ababa is a city of over three million people, located quite near the very center of Ethiopia; more specifically, it occupies a high plateau over 8,000 feet above sea level, which gives it its usually-temperate climate, and stands above Lake Koka to its southeast, and to the west of the famous Awash River, which bifurcates the country. It is the seat of the African Union, the United Nations headquarters for the Economic Commission for Africa, and one of the civic and cultural centers for the eastern continent.

The Metropolitan Police Headquarters stood near the center of downtown, just a few blocks from the Ministry of Justice; it was an ultra-modern building with a stylish facade, and inside was everywhere glass and light tinted alloys, futuristic designs and complex security procedures that suggested a futuristic vision.

On July 2nd Janan checked with the day watch commander to find the investigating officers in the Mgbato case, and luck was with her, as both men were in the building, at their desks in the Homicide department. Jeilu Panolo was the senior man, a 12-year veteran who had worked in homicide for six years; his junior partner, Assefa Kamada, had joined the force five years earlier, and was but one year in Homicide.

Assefa was clearly attracted to Janan from the first, and more than willing to spend time with her. "Oh, we were assigned the case by the minister himself," he claimed with a proud grin. "And this, even though some of us have already dealt with the Tahaku tribe."

"Really?" Janan leaned closer, all attention.

"Why do you think that was?"

"I assume it was due to our closure rate," Jeilu said, a little more somberly. "Assefa and I have closed some 90% of our cases, the highest percentage in the department—and, three-quarters of our cases have led on to conviction."

"That many," she confirmed, trying not to sound overly impressed, which she wasn't. "And, you were assigned the case the same day was brought into custody?"

"No, the day after," Jeilu said. "Captain Makota spoke did speak first with Osei Negash on that same day of the murder."

"Did Osei turn it down?"

"I can't think why he would," said Jeilu as he called up the case file on his computer. "He isn't from the Tahaku tribe, and so far as we're aware he knew none of the principals involved."

Janan consulted her notepad. "So, as I understand it, you and Assefa were first to interview the victim's wife...?"

"Yes, Ms. Takelo ; it was she who found the body."

"It was she that directed us to Otah Mgbato—she and her sister witnessed the confrontation that occurred between Ngbato and Alemu two days before."

"So, you two went to Ngbato's home, found him there, and he agreed to accompany you here?"

Jeilu sipped his coffee. "We had to wait for him to shut down his email, but he went with us voluntarily."

Her interest piqued. "Did you glance at his email?"

"We had no cause at the time."

"He was a person of interest," Assafa said, "That's why we brought him in for questioning."

But Jeilu shook his head. "That would be an invasion of privacy," he told her.

"And, you didn't consider compelling him to come in for questioning invasive?"

"It's all in how you look at it—anyway, Ngbato was not under arrest until after his interview."

"When was his server secured?"

"The following day, maybe—you would need to verify that with Technical Inquiries."

"I see...well, thank you."

Assefa then inched closer to her. "There's much more we can tell you about the case," he claimed, smiling. "You could come by tomorrow, the next day...we could discuss it all over breakfast."

She smiled. "I do need to know more about Mgbato's interview—you could just tell me now."

"Oh, but tomorrow I'll be better dressed."

"Don't count on that," Jeilu cautioned. "what he's wearing now is about the best he has."

"Then, I'll go shopping tonight and buy new," Assefa promised.

"You look just fine," she said, and turned to go. "One question more—do you know whether Captain Hagos has a history with the Tahaku tribe?"

"Aren't you the curious one," Assefa noted. "He hasn't mentioned any connection to the tribe, and I've known our captain for over ten years; he's a good, honest man. You can take him at his word."

"That's good to know...thank you."

Captain Hagos was in his small, sparse office when Janan came to his door; he waved her in, and set down the report he was reviewing.

"Please, sit down," he said with a welcoming gesture. "I understand you've caught the case of Nega Alemu, you and Ojo Teferra...how can I help?"

"Did you initially plan to send Detective Negash on the investigation?"

"I did," he confirmed; then, "Why do you ask?"

"Why didn't you assign him the case?"

"He knows the victim's family," Hagos told her. "one of his cousins is married to the sister-in-law of the victim; Negash is a fine detective, but I wanted to avoid any conflict of interest, so I decided to err on the side of caution."

She updated her notes. "Has he spoken to you concerning the case?"

"No; and, he never requested involvement—my detectives know their protocols, Ms. Takelo, and they know how best to secure a conviction. We are disciplined and well-trained here."

"And, your detectives Ngbato placed under arrest once he failed to produce an alibi?"

He nodded. "They considered him a risk for flight."

"Why? They found him at home half an hour after the killing—he was virtually waiting for them there."

"He has an assault charge in his past; so, he must have expected his past might weigh against him."

She considered this. "Is Detective Negash here today?"

"He is not; he has a summer cold, just as my young ones do—it's making the rounds, you know."

"I'll be mindful," Janan promised. "Thank you, captain."

When she returned to the Ministry Ojo was making his own notes, these in regard to the deposed statements during and directly after Ngbato's interview and subsequent arrest. He offered her coffee, which he'd just brewed, and she couldn't accept fast enough. "Ngbato seems to have cooperated fully with investigators," he mentioned, scrolling down the files on screen. "He doesn't deny the argument two days prior—in fact, he does into some detail about it, including admitting that he said Alemu would pay for what he'd done."

"He actually meant, what Alemu failed to do." She stirred in g good lot of cream into her coffee, and she noticed that Ojo noticed. "If you put enough stuff in it, you don't need to pay the high prices for those specialty coffees."

"Until it's no longer coffee," he said.

"And, your point is…?" Janan smiled, and sat. "Mgbako's behavior was certainly curious."

"What did you learn from the investigators?"

"That I have a more suspicious mind than they," she huffed. "They had a chance to review his email account when he was detained; it was up, it was in plain view…they didn't do it."

Ojo shrugged. "I suppose they knew the tech department could retrieve it."

"And, Captain Hagos has a detective in the precinct with a connection to the Tahaku tribe—he didn't assign him the case; Hagos cites a possible conflict of interest."

Ojo paused. "Is he working it tangentially?"

"I don't know, I haven't spoken with him yet." She quickly added, "He has a cold."

"It may not have any relevance, but we need to know all we can—call him, ask him about the case, see what he says." He sat back. "I've arranged for our first interview with Otah Ngbato at the jail—the tribe has hired Mohammed Seboka to defend him."

"He specializes in tribal law, not capital cases," Janan said.

"You're familiar with him?"

Janan nodded. "I faced him once in court over a fraud charge—he won."

"What were the charges?"

"A local swindler was selling necklaces to tourists that he claimed had magical properties—and maybe they did, since he was acquitted."

"If you bought any of those magic necklaces we could use them for this case," Ojo told her. "A grieving son, taking out vengeance on a charlatan medicine man he blamed for his mother's death...he might elicit sympathy in the jury."

"And he didn't run, and he cooperated with authorities...do you think he'll claim justification?"

"If he does, then where's the murder weapon—it being missing is the strongest argument for consciousness of guilt."

"Unless he really is innocent," Janan said.

"We'll ask him tomorrow. 1 pm—gather together a list of questions for him, and we'll review them in the morning. I'll be leaving mid-afternoon today, I have shopping to do."

She smiled. "You do the shopping?"

"It's my turn, she did the shopping before we were married."

Janan looked at Afia's picture atop his file cabinet—even in this random casual photograph, she looked like she belonged on the cover of some fashion magazine. "What is she like?"

"She's magic," Ojo said, and Janan partly believed him. "I'm picking up wine, among other things—I'll pick up one for you, if you'd like."

"What makes you think I drink," she asked.

"All lawyers drink," Ojo claimed. "It's the only way we can face ourselves."

"Then, I'll take a white."

"What's your birr limit?" The birr is the paper currency in Ethiopia, roughly equivalent to one U.S. dollar.

"Thirty; for a zinfindel, if they have one."

"Fifty, it is," Ojo said with a smile.

The mid-afternoon traffic was nowhere near as brutal as the previous day's rush hour, and Ojo arrived at Edjeta's Market calm and relaxed; but even midday and midweek, the store was crowded, and shoppers pushy and prickly from the summer heat. Edjeta's Market was one of the biggest in the district, and close to the famous Merkato, the great open-air market.

Ojo had in cart some necessaries and three bottles of wine, one of course for Janan, and was three shoppers in line from the cashier when he heard his name. "Ojo, is that you?"

He turned. Afia's friend Inaya Tafa was in the line parallel to his, with a full cart of her own. He grinned warmly. "Good afternoon, Inaya—how are you? It's brave of you to come out in this heat."

"There are some things you cannot do without for long," she said, and glanced at his wine-biased cart. "I'll not say more!"

"Oh, I won't finish them *all* before I get home," he kidded. "How are you doing, how is Upendo—he is nine now, yes?"

"Only just," Inaya said. She was a thin, lanky woman with very short hair, and wore a loose bright-printed blouse with an amethyst-colored necklace. "And he is so smart, he may be skipping a grade this next year."

"I am not at all surprised," Ojo replied warmly.

After checking out the two walked together to their cars, both parked under canopy to avoid the sun. "I'll be certain to call Afia very soon," Inaya said, as she unloaded her cart. "I feel somehow embarrassed, awkward—I mean, I haven't seen her since our movie night, the night her father passed."

"I don't know why you should feel awkward for that reason," he told her. "There was no way of knowing he would pass away that night."

""No; but still, she and I taking in a film, when he...oh, you know what I'm trying to say.'

"I do; and, it's no reason to feel you should avoid her. You two are old friends, and I know she'd want to hear from you; and if you don't call, she will."

"I know," Inaya said.

"I'll return your cart for you," Ojo offered.

"It is very good to see you."

"Thank you, that's most kind," she said. "and I hope Afia is quite over her illness."

He stopped. "How do you mean?"

"The stomach illness," Inaya said. "That night, it bothered her so badly, we had to leave the film before it ended, she had become so nauseous."

Ojo paused before speaking—he knew nothing of this; in fact, Afia told him that she and Inaya discussed the film afterward, which was why she came home so late that night. "Did you and Afia talk about the film?"

"Not at all," Inaya told him. "We usually do, it's almost a ritual with us—but Afia was ill, she said she was going home right away."

He nodded. "She is feeling much better," he quickly said as cover. "Whatever it was, was temporary...I'll tell her I saw you."

"And, please tell her I am not avoiding her, that I'll talk with her this week. Thank you again, Ojo, and drive carefully."

"You, as well—and stay cool, Inaya." Ojo put in his groceries, but once in the car just froze. Why would Afia lie, did she lie? And for what possible reason—surely, nothing to do with the film she attended with Inaya...but what, *what* did this mean? He had been still for only a minute, but even under canopy he soon felt too warm, and started the car, and its air conditioning. It was a short drive home from Edjeta's Market, and through it all Ojo questioned why such a simple omission didn't line up, why Afia said nothing about an hour or so missing from her personal history, and whether she lied to Inaya, or to him, or both.

Nothing was said about the market encounter at dinner that evening, though it preoccupied Ojo all the while—Afia for her part mistook his quiet for concern over the Ngbato case, and finally said as much. "You are right to worry over it, it's your first murder case," she said to him. "And from what you've said it presents some difficulties, does it not?"

"We may be in over our heads," he said.

"Not you," she said with a warm smile.

"Honey, I don't know about Ms. Takelo, but not you; you will prevail, I know it."

"I saw Inaya Tafa today at the market," he told her offhandedly. "She mentioned that you haven't spoken since the night your father died."

"We have been so busy," she quickly said.

"I imagine, we've both been busy—I certainly hope she knows, there is no intent behind it."

"I don't—"

"Was she upset," Afia asked, as she opened one of the new bottles of wine. "She can't hide her feelings not at all, if she's upset, she shows it."

"She isn't angry with you," Ojo reported.

"She mentioned it, rather in passing."

"I'll call her tonight, after dinner—i hadn't realized that so much time had passed."

That wasn't like Afia, either—she was thoughtful of her friends, almost to vigilance; Ojo hoped she would add something, but she didn't.

Finally he said, "I'm sure she'll appreciate that."

She poured two glasses of wine. "Is there anything specific that you'd like to discuss, concerning your case?"

"Perhaps," Ojo replied, so wrapped up in questions that he almost felt inhibited when he took the glass from her.

Three.

Afia was shortly out of her shower when her phone rang. "Inaya, good morning—you're up early…yes, I did. Oh, very much better, thank you—it has passed, whatever it was…no. No, I don't think so—well, I am late…did I—no, in part because I wasn't all that fond of it. You did? You're more sentimental than I—I'm not so, well, trusting, let's say…I don't know, around here somewhere, probably downstairs. When—next week? I'd love to, and do we include—I'll ask, I'm not sure, what with this new case…we'll see.

Thank you so much for checking, I hope—yes, I hope I didn't worry you at all then. I will, and a long hug for Upendo…yes, 'bye."

Once she concluded the call Afia sat on her bed, and gave a quick glance at the clock; she had plenty of time, no problem…Something Inaya said got her thinking back to her childhood—a strange childhood, as her parents started her being photographed at twelve years old. She was a Friday child (hence her name), tall and lanky in early school, good at the tall girl sports like volleyball, always captain, always with deference.

She didn't know that little girl now, wouldn't know her should they pass along some narrow pebbled way in the summer sun…and, all she'd done in those middle years, always directed here, there, different cities in different countries, foreign languages, but always the same pressures, the push, the stares…

Afia chose an isolate position in Archives, not to be alone, but to feel protected; and maybe there was some of that in her marriage, too. Ojo was 'her Ojo'—she'd often said it in public, at functions or among friends, and never heard a single objection, so proud was he to be with her, perhaps even just to know her. It was rare—he was, she thought; and he, too, is to be protected.

The following afternoon Ojo and Janan arrived at the Municipal Jail to interview Otah Mgbako—his attorney Mohammed Seboka sat beside him, well-dressed and oozing self-confidence, if not necessarily confidence in his client. They greeting the prosecutors in the Interview Room, and Seboka spoke first. "I have reviewed your case against my client, and all I see are smoke and mirrors," he claimed. "All you have is motive, and motive is not admissible as an evidentiary element."

"You may need to polish those mirrors," Ojo countered. "We have witnesses to Mr. Mgbako expressing intent to harm, opportunity, and no verifiable alibi—if your client wishes to expand on his original statement, we're here to listen."

"So you can use his own words against him?" Seboka adjusted his glasses. "That's a favor he can do without."

"He claims he was at home watching television at the time of the crime," Janan said. "he must realize, that is no alibi at all."

"It is the truth," Mgbako asserted. He was a young man, not yet twenty of age, with short curled hair and stubble. "I can tell you what happened in the film I was watching."

"Please, Mr. Mgbako—that information is easily obtained online," Ojo told him. "If you had made a phone call from home around that hour, or had you been on your computer, that electronic signature could place you; otherwise…"

"And, the film you cited has been on television before," Janan reminded him.

"So, you seek to convict my client for his taste in movies?" Seboka drew a paper from his jacket. "I want my client released on his own recognizance, as you have no direct evidence against him—this is a copy of the request to the District Court."

"He's not leaving here," Janan asserted. "He's suspect in a capital crime."

"Mr. Mgbako is unjustly accused, and I believe the judges will see that for themselves."

"I did not do this thing," his client repeated.

"I admit, I was not sorry to hear he was dead, but I had nothing to do with it."

Seboka motioned him quiet. "We will let our motion speak for him; til then, I've advised my client to keep silent."

"That may not be sound advice," Janon told Mgbako, who'd fixed his attention on her.

"If what you tell us is exculpatory, that will help your case."

"And a simple denial will do you no good," Oja added. "If you have more to tell us, now is the time."

"No; now is not the time," Seboka said. "If Mr. Mgbako has more to say, he will say it before a presiding judge."

Janan leaned nearer to him. "Otah, have you more to say?"

He motioned, as if to speak—but a quick touch from his attorney quieted him. "I am sorry," he told her.

"We will see you at the hearing," Saboka told them, and he and his client left the room; once Mgbako had returned to his cell, his attorney spoke further. "Remember, you must not talk to anyone about your case without my being present, do you understand?-You're volunteering to speak just now might work against us."

"I was only telling the truth."

But Saboka shook his head. "This is not about the truth, this is about securing your freedom—you say you're innocent, fine; but, your protestations alone will sway no-one."

"How can that be?"

His lawyer sighed. "This isn't a schoolyard, you're not a child—the state is accusing you; and whatever what were taught, this playing-field is not level."

Ojo spoke once he and Janan left the jail. "A shark like Seboka does not work for chum…Janan, find out who's paying his fee."

"Mgbako wanted to talk to us, you could see it," she said. "Why didn't Seboka let him speak?

He's young, but he wouldn't be so foolish as to incriminate himself."

"Saboka isn't a criminal attorney, and when you faced him he was defending con men—maybe, he thinks his clients are better off quiet."

"And maybe, he knows something we don't."

"That wouldn't take much," Ojo remarked.

"We should know about Mgbako's family, his mother's illness, and just what transpired between her family and the victim. Tribal elders check into hospitals all the time, and so do medicine men—we need to know why Mgbako's mother refused standard cancer treatments."

She agreed in principle, but added a wrinkle. "Medical records are confidential, Ojo."

"For now we don't need her case history, just a general profile; and the names of her doctors are not privileged. Talk to them, and see if they can shed light on why Kande Mgbato refused further treatment."

First Janan wanted to speak with Detective Baka Negash, who was now returned to duty after being sidelined by a summer cold. Well, true, he had returned to the precinct, but he was not yet well. "Two weeks—two weeks this crud has lingered," he sniffled, papers, files and whatnot covering his desk. "Colds are supposed to last only a week; ten days, if you're unlucky..."

"Maybe it's the flu," Janan suggested.

"I've had my shots," he told her. "it's supposed to keep you from catching the flu."

She smiled. "Actually, it's supposed to lessen the severity of the virus."

He gave her a look. "Whose side are you on?"

She didn't know quite how to answer that.

"I'm here concerning the Alemu case—I understand, you discussed it with Captain Hagos..."

He said he had. "I have a cousin, who's married into the Tahaku—I knew Nega and Kaji Alumu slightly, through my cousin; I also knew how deeply Nega distrusted modern medicine, and promoted his herbal and dietary remedies instead, which sometimes didn't end well."

"Tahaku medical practices are subject to review by the Ministry of Health," Janan said.

"Were any complaints filed?"

"I had them fooled, I think—when someone got sicker in his care, he claimed it was "God's will', or so my cousin told me. She had the common sense to visit clinics when she felt ill."

"So, his remedies never worked?"

He daubed his nose with tissues. "Some must have, or Chief Nissanke would have dismissed him—I'm sorry I couldn't have seen him about this cold."

"Are you taking vitamin C?"

"I've taken so much vitamin C, I now have a lifelong immunity to scurvy!"

Janan smiled. "I don't think it works that way."

"I'll say this, Ms. Takelo—I understand why Otah Ngbato would have been so angry."

"Very well; thank you." Before she left him Janan said, "It's only a few more days, detective."

"You could mean that either way," he claimed.

That afternoon Ojo was ostensibly reviewing the witness statements, but his thoughts were on Afia and her lie. There was no upcoming occurrence that would explain a deviation from routine, no birthday, anniversary or holiday that would account for secrecy, and even if there were the timing was wrong, the hour or so in question being so late.

Was this evidence of an affair? The lateness of the hour or so in question was suggestive, but practicality argued against it—Afia worked an 8am to 5pm shift at the Archives, and was nearly always home before Ojo on weeknights, sometimes home and already actively engaged in something, and every weekend they were together. Ojo had noticed no changes in Afia's conduct or mood, nothing unusual or troubling til very recently.

Could it be the very start of an affair, though—is it likely that this assignation began that night, coincident with the death of her father? It didn't seem likely; and then, how would such an affair continue, and hope to escape notice? And if not that, how likely would be a prearranged one-time tryst? No; it makes no sense...and if Inaya was lying, if Afia wasn't with her for the film at all, why then invent an anomaly that throws the entire deceit into question?

Ojo had known Afia for six years, and been married to her for three; and in all that time he never had cause to doubt her, or disbelieve her word...and did he, even now? Perhaps Afia had some personal reason for the deception that she's chosen not to disclose, and still might—has she not that right as an individual, to keep some certain aspects of her life private? Was Ojo in the wrong not only to doubt her, but question her behavior so minutely?

He put this all to one side when Janan tapped at his office door. "Kande Mgbato's physician is Dr. Kabaka Beyene, from St.

Mary's Hospital; he had been treating her for the past two years."

Ojo nodded. "And what does he have to say?"

"Virtually nothing," she replied. "He only confirmed that she died of cancer, and that anything more specific is covered by doctor-patient privilege."

"Did you tell him we're inquiring as part of a murder investigation?"

"I did," Janan said. "He was singly unimpressed."

"We need to know more...did you speak to to someone in Oncology?"

"The chief of same, who suggested we could only see Mrs. Mgbato's medical records pursuant to a court order."

"We need her medical history in evidence."

"We also need to know more about the tribal medical practices, and we won't need a court order for that."

Ojo smiled. "If we brought one they'd ignore it...find out who to speak to at the Tahaku tribe, and see if we can establish a pattern of practice for the victim; go there in person, if need be."

"Tribal elders would better respond to a man, Ojo—you should go. I'll fly to Dire Dawa tomorrow, to meet with Mgbato's father; so far, he's visited his son only once since his arrest."

"There could be bad blood between them."

"His father left the family two years ago, and started a new one—he's a mining executive there, so there's some family money; it could be his father is paying Saboka's fee."

"If he is so supportive, why haven't we heard from him? Why doesn't he come here, speak to his son's good character? And if he's reluctant to, how likely is it that his son is innocent?"

"No, that's supposition; there could be a dozen reasons—family dynamics can sometimes remain a mystery, even when you know all there is to know."

"Both families have kept a distance," she noticed.

"It worries me that they haven't been more forthcoming before this."

"I think they're hiding something," Janan said, "something most likely out in the open."

Four.

That evening the questions that pursued Ojo earlier regrouped, and would not be still. He found himself watching Afia for subtle signals or odd behaviors, slip-ups, the way a prosecutor watches a defendant at the defense table; it was a skill in people-reading that took years to master, and in those hours he hated it.

He just ask her, he told himself—and yet, with someone as self-possessed and proud as Afia, who could turn prickly as quickly as a porcupine, the question by itself could do damage, let alone whatever her answer might be. And worse, if she should give an answer he didn't believe, then his doubts would compound, should he dismiss an innocent or neutral explanation.

The trouble with prosecutors, he knew, was their tendency to prosecute.

After work he and Afia braved the endless traffic to visit Bookworld on the Bole Road; the store sold the highest number of English titles in the city (both Ojo and Afia were fluent in English), as well as books in Amharic, French, and Somali. And Bookworld was open until 9pm, to better accommodate those who worked into the early evening.

Afia spent much of her time there in the History section, while Ojo browsed the many Fiction shelves along the far wall—he chose two promising novels, one of them in English, and found his wife in Poetry, and had in hand a new biography of Empress Zauditu. "All these poets are foreigners," she lamented, something she'd bemoaned before. "Why is it we have no great national poets?"

"The language is certainly not lacking in beauty," Ojo said. "Perhaps, that's why—ever notice how many harsh languages boat a surfeit of fine poets, almost like taking up a challenge."

She knit her brows. "There are no harsh languages, Ojo—every language carries a musicality unique to it; that's why poetry is universal. But then some languages don't lend themselves to musicality...Nahuatl comes to mind."

"Poetry aligns with a basic need in language, where vagueness and suggestiveness can be most useful—those instances where concepts are best expressed by metaphor."

She considered a volume of Emily Dickinson.

"I think, it's to better understand the world—or else tell the world, why you've failed to...so, what have you found?"

He shared his choices as they chose seating in the tiny lounge where shoppers could sit and examine their choices; one was Hardy's *Tess on the D'urbervilles*, and the other Gide's *The Counterfeiters*.

"The Gide book is described as 'experimental fiction', which might suggest it's actually factual," Ojo commented, as he paged through. "This French will not be easy-going.'

"The best books are not," Afia replied.

"My English is not much better than your French, which is why I chose Dickinson—although with her, only the language is simple."

"A quiet anarchist, everything just under the surface."

"Yes, exactly!" His aphorism made her smile.

The couple then browsed the art history shelves, and then archaeology, where Afia chose a beautiful picture book on ancient Egypt—as she thumbed through, she marveled at the incredible images of temples, statues, mosaics, all thousands of years old.

Ojo shared her amazement. "We will never know how they accomplished all this," he quietly said, in awe. The Karnak Temple alone is like a miracle in stone."

Afia seemed taken more by the gorgeous paintings of natural scenes still preserved over the eons, their bright colors still vivid and evocative.

"It's almost as though Time never touched them," she softly said. "It's as if their gods were real, and as a gift for their devotion exempted them."

Once the couple arrived home Afia caught up on her emails, sitting beside Ojo. "This new case is worrying you," she noticed. "I can see you tense whenever you return to work on this case...darling, even if you should lose this case, the ministry would not blame you. This is your first capital case."

Ojo didn't respond directly, but opened his own laptop. "We're not getting much cooperation from the parties involved," he said vaguely. "I think Janan needs to push harder." Then he said, "On the other hand, I can't tell her to throw her weight around, since she weighs so little."

"I'll bet she's pretty," she said, sneaking in a hint of jealousy.

He shrugged one shoulder. "You want a pretty prosecutor, it helps you win over the jury."

"You don't need the help," she said.

"Me? I need the Queen of Sheba herself."

Afia took a moment. "So, Janan is pretty, then?"

Ojo grinned. "She is devastating!"

She quickly glanced his way, and when he leaned closer, as if to view her screen, she partly closed it. "Eyes on your own paper," she teased.

Afia had done this bid for privacy before, and he'd thought nothing of it; but tonight Ojo found something darker in it, even though he knew better. His feelings were at odds, and while they riled he found them hard to quiet. He returned to his emails, responding or deleting, and now and then glanced over to his wife, who seemed very much engaged in something—something, and not just reviewing email.

What was it, he wondered, that had her so intently focused, even to biting her lip and mouthing syllables to herself? What was she reading, studying, what caught her up to such a shut exclusion, so rapt and wrapped up as to scarcely notice he was close by? She did look his way now and again, but with a look that said, 'I'm busy just now'.

Or was he reading in, seeing something that wasn't really there? It embarrassed him that he distrusted so quickly over trifles, 'proofs of holy writ', as someone in *Othello* said; Iago, probably, though that might render the statement suspect—not in and of itself, but according to context.

Was Ojo overreacting when he need not react at all?

When she finally closed her laptop Afia wasn't happy. She set it by, drew her long legs in onto the couch, lotus-style, and lost herself in thought. Ojo had finished his email sweep by then, and started a review of phone charges dating back six months—this search revealed nothing unexpected, no unknown numbers repeated with any frequency. In fact, the only number Afia often called was known to him, it was Inaya's number; so, unless she was having an affair with Inaya, this phone search was fruitless.

And Ojo was pretty certain Afia was not in love with Inaya, since she'd known her before she met him—if she was he likely would have noticed, and she'd have married her instead.

That night Afia waited to remove her makeup til later, not that she wore much; and as she wiped down her face, she caught her husband watching her from the doorway. "Actors have to do this," she mentioned. "I think male actors probably feel more affinity with women because of it, don't you think?"

"Only God would know," Ojo said lightly.

"Yes; only God could know."

"On the other hand, the short lifespans of celebrity marriages argue against actors' simpatico with the women they marry."

Afia looked a bit confused. "So—maybe just unsuccessful actors?"

"Who have to apply their own makeup," he concluded, with some verbal flourish.

She daubed her lipstick on some tissue. "I love having so smart a husband."

"I could make more money," he said.

"We both could," she agreed. "but we're all right—we're lucky to both be working, the economy being as it is…" When she moved to brush past, she rested her hand near his heart.

"You still look at me like a suitor," she told him.

"It still feels like our first date," Ojo said.

Afia kissed him. "It still is our first date."

Five.

Tahaku Village was the home of the Tahaku tribe, situated not very far from Addis Ababa—it somewhat resembled a poorer township, with small houses mixed in with thatched *gochos* and traditional mud huts, though those huts were not homes but used mainly for storage and some ceremonial purposes. The Tahaku numbered over 4,000, with some members having moved to neighboring cities, but still close to the village.

Ojo drove to the Tahaku on Thursday morning before the heat got too bad; the village surroundings were flat open land and low hills, but extended to within three miles of the famous Awash River—it was not unusual for villagers to see antelope or ibex wander into town, for flamingos to come visit, and only last month a family of zebras were fed and fussed over as they passed through the center streets.

Ojo had come to speak with Kaji Alemu, the widow of Nega Alemu ; she lived in one of the nicer houses in the village, as befitted the tribal healer. Kaji was middle-aged and just starting to grey, she wore loose western-style clothes and a traditional Tahaku necklace, beaded with turquoise. "I had gone to meet with Apala Nogu, who lives just across the way," Kaji told Ojo over coffee. "She and I had agreed to talk that afternoon about textiles."

"Textiles?"

"We both embroider," she explained. "We fashion shawls, sashes, headbands, that we offer for sale either here in the village, or in the city.

So, we had met together for no more than one half hour, and I returned home—that's when I found my husband dead on the living room floor."

"This was between 2pm and 2:30," Ojo asked, and she confirmed it. "And, the police came within fifteen minutes."

"It was awful," she said, with a little quiver.

"When they asked if I knew of anyone who carried malice towards Nega, I mentioned Mgbato—I was reluctant to do so, but they would have learned about him soon anyway, once they asked around the village."

Ojo sipped his coffee. "I understand that you and your sister both witnessed the confrontation two days prior, between your husband and Mgbato."

"Apala was also a witness—she saw it, too."

He noted this. "And, you know of no-one else who held any animus toward—uh, who bore any ill will towards your husband?"

"I see what you do," she said, patiently.

"You wish to see if my answers are the same, as when I spoke with the police that day...well, yes, one person I know did carry a grudge against Nega—Juba Toko, who complained that cheated her on a mixture of herbal medicines. Juba is 90 years old, Mr. Teferra , and very nearly bedridden."

"When you called for help, did you call from your house phone?"

"No, I called from my cell."

He glanced to the house phone, quite nearby in the living room. "I see; did you carry your cell phone to your meeting with Apala?"

"I always carry my cell phone with me."

"We all do now, I suppose."

"Certainly—we are traditional here, not backward; I called 991, then called our chieftain."

He glanced to his notebook. "Did your husband own any ceremonial artifacts that he kept in the home?"

"Certainly; his family line stretches back over three hundred years... Nega owned many traditional pieces, some very valuable; in fact, I have in the den on display a warrior's spear and shield from almost 300 years ago, handed down through generations—would you care to see them?"

"Very much," Ojo said, and she led him to the den; there in a glass case were the antique feather-crested spear, and the richly-decorated full-body shield, the ornate designs on its front from a language now lost. "These are very beautiful, Kaji—I imagine they've valuable."

"I find them comforting," Kaji said to him.

"They call to mind a simpler, purer time in Africa's history, the times of the Masai, the great power of the warrior-classes who fought for their beliefs—these days we compromise, we sue; we fade away."

On her lunch hour Afia met with Inaya by prearrangement; the two had agreed on dining at The Perfect Circle, a restaurant very near Afia's workplace, very familiar to her. And while women dressed for the weather, one of them looked like she could be meeting with the prime minister.

"Most of the men in here have noticed you," Inaya mentioned as they awaited their orders.

"Doesn't it get tiring?"

"It's not important," Afia said. "In fact that's one reason I quit modeling—you have no control, you work for the agency; I had no say about representing this product, or that company, no matter their business practices or records on the environment, because I was a product, too."

When their orders came she added, "Also, I was 23, and soon to age out."

For a moment Inaya thought that a joke, then realized it was not. "Ojo never asked you to leave the modeling?"

"Do you mean, was he jealous?" Afia started on her seafood salad, and smiled. "When we started he said something like, 'Jealousy will have to be my life's burden', something like that; it was sweet. So I told him that if I do stray, I'll make sure he never, ever finds out."

"So you meant you'll never stray, since he's so clever he would find out…it's an odd reassurance."

"I never have," Afia said lightly, "and I don't plan to."

"You're lucky to have each other."

"Inaya, I need—I want to ask you about your meeting with him the other night."

"With Ojo?" Inaya tried her beef and noodle dish, which she found surprisingly good.

"What about it?"

"I know you told him about my not feeling well—what else did you tell him?"

"What else would I tell him? What else was there to tell?"

"Did you mention—"

"I didn't tell him how poor the film was," Inaya interjected. "You know, I was almost grateful we left early—that actor I like so much is usually more reliable than that."

Afia smiled that dazzling killer smile that could bend Time, that Afia could use any time she wanted. "Actors miss—even rich, famous actors; sometimes, that's endearing."

Inaya agreed. "No, I told Ojo you weren't well, I could see that...you went home, you said we'd talk later; and, we did. That was all...why?"

"He's acting strangely," she confided, thinking it through. "It's little things, like, well, you know with Upendo. I don't quite see it."

She looked concerned. "Is he angry?"

"No, more—more unsettled, I would say."

"Maybe it's this murder case?"

Afia's lovely dark eyes lit. "Yes! No doubt, it's this murder case...certainly."

Meanwhile Janan arrived at Dire Dawa Airport shortly before noon. Dire Dawa is the country's second-largest city, and known for its flourishing industries and modern railway line. Janan took a taxi to the Gessesse Building to meet with Tamirat Mgbako in his midtown office. "I don't know how much I can tell you," Tamirat said from his c-shaped glass desk. "Otah's mother and I split up nearly three years ago, and I've seen Otah only a handful of times since...I did see him last week, of course, at the jail."

"Are you paying for his attorney?"

He nodded. "The Tahaku are generous, but not very well-off—I offered to augment a fund they had started, then decided to return their donations to them. I can certainly afford to front my own son's defense."

She glanced around her, to the tasteful and affluent office. "So, you believe then in his innocence?"

"I cannot say; I was not there."

His reply surprised her. "Do you think he's capable of killing someone?"

Tamirat sighed. "Otah has always had a temper," he said, "He assaulted a schoolmate when he was a teenager; the other boy required eight stitches."

"There was no police report," Janan said.

No report was made, he explained. "Some ordinances are more lax for native tribes like the Tahaku—no charges were filed, and the medical report was filed under 'nuisance'; no more was made of it. The boys became friends later on."

"We may need your permission to access family medical records, Mr. Mgbato—was your ex-wife treated solely at St. Mary's Hospital?"

"Not exclusively, Kande was also treated at the Augustine Clinic; and she has a sister named Abiba, she may be able to tell you more about the medical history. She lives in Kenya."

"Your son's trial begins next month," she told him. "You'll likely be called to testify."

"I'll make myself available," Tanirat said.

That Friday Ojo left the Ministry for the day mid-afternoon, as he often did on Fridays, and arrived home some time before he expected Afia.

He retrieved the mail, and as he sorted noticed a registered letter addressed to Afia from the Office of the Precinct Medical Examiner—he paused, as he suspected what it was, and included the letter with her other mail. He then thumbed through his own, and seeing nothing urgent started to prepare the evening meal; that was the house arrangement, that the first one home prepared the dinner.

When Afia arrived home Ojo was in the kitchen in his casual clothes, manning a simmering pot of rice. "I'm mixing in chicken, bell peppers, black olives, zucchini and onions," he told her as she stopped by for a quick kiss. "I call it 'Chicken Afia'."

"Oh, but will it come when you call it?" She slipped off her business jacket, and kicked off her shoes. "I had a day full of documents, and by about 2 o'clock they all looked the same, like in Kafka."

He glanced over, still stirring peppers and onions. "I've read only *Metamorphosis*."

She unbuttoned a little. "In *The Castle* entrants are given copies of different forms to complete, ostensibly for different reasons—only, all the questions on the forms are the same."

"I brought in the mail," he continued. "and you received a notice from the Medical Examiner's office."

"Oh?" Afia turned.

"It's in with your other mail," Ojo told her.

She refrained from opening her mail til after dinner, then used her silvered letter opener (fussy as she was)—the notice from the Medical Examiner was as expected, the determination of Kashka Selassie 's death. The examiner determined Afia's father died 'natural of causes ...related to cardiac arhythmia'.

Afia quickly put her hand to her face upon reading this, and kept her expression hid for some seconds—her eyes welled with tears, and after sever moments she set the letter down, but kept her gaze on it. She then turned her face away from Ojo, who was just to her right side, and gave out a sigh.

"I'm sorry; perhaps I should have opened the letter," Ojo said.

"No, no..." She took another visible breath, then looked at him. "It's as we all thought, a heart attack. My father died of natural causes."

He looked over the letter. "We'll want to keep this somewhere safe."

Afia quickly took it from him. "I'll do it—I'll place it in our lock box. And, you're right, that we'll need this in future." She then ignored her remaining missives and went upstairs to their bedroom, where they kept the lock box.

It was odd behavior—at least, Ojo thought so. Afia was not one for tears, having cried only a handful of times in all the years he'd known her; even when she was told her father had died, she was upset, but she didn't cry. And odd too, that she covered her expression at her reading the letter, covered so well her expression could not be read hardly at all...and while it was an emotional moment, Ojo knew that gesture to be unlike her.

Of course, grief effects everyone uniquely, and the loss of a parent is a deeply personal thing—and, Ojo did not know Afia when her mother passed away...still, she and her father were not very close, and were in fact somewhat at odds over the past couple of years, his seeming disappointment in her taking a job in civil service, when he expected Afia's natural beauty and poise could have made her a celebrity—in truth, Ojo had thought so, too.

"The notice is secure," Afia announced, as she returned downstairs. "I've placed it in a plastic sleeve."

Ojo sat on the couch. "This weekend, we—"

"Sunday is the reading of the will," Afia reminded, somewhat tersely, then spoke rapidly as if annoyed. "We need to be in Kobo Sebese's office at 2 o'clock."

"I know; we will be." He kept his eyes on her as she returned to her remaining mail, none of which seemed of much importance. "So, have we won the lottery?"

"We don't play the lottery," she calmly said, with an impatient glance. "and if we do not play, then how could we be expected to win?"

"I hadn't thought of that," Ojo said, but he could see her relax as she made her long remark.

She then sat next to him. "I thought you lawyers thought of everything—was I sold a bill of goods?"

"I would think you'd know by now," he lightly replied, and let his gaze travel away from hers, in hopes that she see no more than he wished to show.

Six.

The reading of Kashka Selassie's will occurred at 2pm on Sunday in the office of Kobo Sobese, Kashka's attorney; present were Ojo and Afia, as well as Kashka's four cousins, and the wives of three of them—luckily this was a spacious office, and though some people had to stand, Sobese thoughtfully assured them that the primary will was short, and contained only one codicil. Once amenities were met, he got down to specifics.

"As you all know, Kashka Selassie was a relatively wealthy man, his cumulative worth having reached over 200,00 dirr; he and I worked on the writing and amending of his will over several months, this final draft having been completed only six months prior to his passing—just last month, as we met over other matters, I asked if he was content with the will in its present state, and he was." Once he read out the read the preamble to the Ethiopian Orthodox template, he came to the heart of the matter.

"Item 1: To my beloved daughter and only child, for whom and in whom I have placed my loving care, and has never and could never disappoint me, I leave my dear Afia one half of my estate, in funds, investments and property, to dispose as she sees fit and proper. We have not always seen eye to eye, we have seen our world in different ways; but she could never know how truly proud I am of her—that these thirty years, she has always been a source of joy to me.

"Item 2…"

Ojo glanced to his wife, who was again in tears, and again not wanting to be seen at that moment; he held her hand, and she squeezed his, as she soon regained her composure. The subsequent bequests were awarded to the four surviving cousins, who received equal shares of the remaining half of Kashka's estate.

"There is a codicil to the will," Sobese said, and once more had the room's full attention.

"Kashka Selassie wished that 10,000 dirr be donated to the poor living in Addis Ababa, the city where Kashka was born and raised; this amount will be divested in equal measure from the individual bequests…and with that, the reading of the will is concluded."

Coffees and biscuits were served after, and Ojo and Afïa visited with the cousins for some time, mostly sharing stories about Kashka—ceremonies concerning a loved one's passing are often less somber affairs than in most western societies, and tend more to celebrate the life that had been than to mourn its loss.

But, in the car on the drive home, Afia's kindness froze. "One half," she snipped, sharp edges on her words. "My father never saw his cousins, never mentioned them, not to me—and *they* receive one half of his estate!"

"Kashka had been ill for some time," Ojo said. "It could be, they interacted more in his later months—and perhaps, he had no reason to mention this to you."

She didn't seem to hear him. "After taxes, we'll receive less than 80,000 birr—perhaps, just over 70,000." Then said, "And, it will take time."

He looked at her. "So?"

Afia was quiet a moment, composing herself.

"It's not important," she quietly said, as they turned down Hegue Taitu Street. "I expected better of him."

"Clearly, you expected more," he corrected.

She gave him an odd look of reproach. "You have never lost a parent—you don't know how I feel."

"Tell me," he urged her. "It isn't emotionally healthy to bottle up your feelings, especially strong ones."

"It is also futile to burden someone else with expressing emotions that change nothing," she tersely retorted. "How I feel won't bring him back, won't change the present; and to be honest, most likely not the future, either."

He cautiously merged into the dense highway traffic. "It's important to have an outlet, Afia—it's another way of showing strength."

"I was raised to bend with the wind," Afia quietly said, so lowly some words were indistinct.

"You bend, so you don't break—and I told you before, I never saw my mother cry…not once."

As they drove on Ojo could tell the subject was now closed; she'd shut and bolted the door to it. He had no business questioning this, either—it was her father and her inheritance, that she could spend it feeding antelope, if she so chose…yet, this was at the last something beyond the central point. This behavior was unusual for her, as had been other moods and motions of late. Ojo was increasingly certain there was something to it beyond the death of her father…but what?

The heat wave which had marred the last nine days had finally subsided, and the city was more like itself that afternoon—and by early evening so was Afia, her mood having passed and her natural playfulness again ascendant. She even challenged Ojo to playing *gabata* that evening, this being a board game similar to backgammon; and when she suggested they play for money, Ojo referred to her inheritance.

"No, no—we only play for your money," she teased, to which he agreed; they'd done this before, and she always won. Their understanding was, were Afia to lose, she'd pay in some other way—and remarkably, she never seemed to lose.

And sometimes she'd 'pay up', even so.

"Do you remember our first kiss," she asked, perhaps to throw him off his game, since Ojo was just a mere mortal. "Do you recall how it happened?"

"I remember wondering how hard you might hit me," Ojo claimed.

She moved her next piece. "You had bought me a necklace with an emerald centerpiece," she said. "Quite cautious of you, since your hands were around my throat at the time!"

"You could have still kneed me.""

"I do recall that you didn't say I was beautiful—that won you points." And as she said that she took five points on the *gabata* board.

"Did I tell you I loved you?"

"It was just our third date!"

"Well, then it couldn't have been true yet… so tell me, am I ever going to win at this game?"

"It's fate, Ojo; you're not meant to win," she said.

The next day Ojo met with Janan in his office to discuss pretrial strategy, and Ojo's impending meeting with the police investigators, and he also said he'd be out of the office in the mid-afternoon on a separate matter.

That afternoon Ojo drove to the Imperial Theater, where Afia and Inaya attended the film the night of Kashka Selassie's death—from there, Ojo drove to Kashka's house, then drove to his own home. Ojo knew when the film played that night, and how long it should have taken Afia to drive directly home, as she told Inaya she intended to do. Even accounting for the different time of day, the experiment gave Afia possibly twenty minutes at her father's home, had she gone there.

Of course, there were several other possibilities—but, there was this one.

And that evening Ojo checked the lock box he and his wife kept in the bedroom; sure enough, the notice of the natural death ruling there there—but, it was not on top, as it should have been, but underneath Afia's birth certificate.

Why would this be, unless both documents were taken out and then replaced this way?

When he returned downstairs Afia was not on her laptop, like she almost always was, especially lately; she was reading a biography of Zauditu, the controversial empress so instrumental in establishing Christian influence in Ethiopia during the early 20th Century. Afia's laptop was right by her on the glass table, and while Ojo sat nearby and read a novel, he noticed her glance at the laptop several times, as if wanting to log on.

"It's nice to have a quiet night," he finally said, quietly.

She smiled. "Is it a good book?"

His expression said, so-so. "It's about time travel, but the author is no H.G. Wells."

She shook her head in disapproval. "Those stories about submarines and circumnavigating balloons, they are too unbelievable."

"No, that was Jules Verne; and, no-one could have guessed what was coming."

She closed her book. "Have you ever thought about which time you'd like to visit? I have, of course, or I wouldn't have brought it up."

Now, Ojo closed his. "What time would you travel to?"

"Well, the 'butterfly effect' notwithstanding, I'd like to visit ancient Egypt, perhaps the building of the pyramids, or the Temple of Karnak—it would be wonderful to see; of course, not speaking the language might prove a problem."

"Were you to visit Akhetaten, you could be mistaken for Nefertiti," he suggested.

The idea appealed to her. "That could have its advantages, couldn't it?" Afia returned to her book, and he to his, though now and then he noticed her sneaking quick glances at her laptop.

The following day Ojo spent his lunch break at Shewa Federal Insurance, where both his and the Selassie family accounts were held. There he spoke with Nahan Skoba, who was Kashka's agent. "I'm not certain I can discuss particulars with you," Skoba said. "There are privacy issues to be considered, even after a client's passing."

Ojo understood. "However, I am not only your client's son-in-law, but also a district prosecutor—if I request a court order, it gives me access to all records connected with the branch, and I don't know if your bosses would welcome that.'

Skoba had called up the Selassie file, before Ojo had finished speaking. I have the records here, what would you like to know?"

"Who is the beneficiary of Kashka's life insurance policy?"

"The principle beneficiary is his daughter, Afia Selassie."

"What is the benefit?"

"The policy is worth 300,000 birr, of which she receive 90%—this originally would have gone to his Kashka' wife, Ilori, but unfortunately she passed away." Did Afia know of the change in the policy? "Oh, yes—Afia was notified shortly after Ilori's passing."

"And, has my wife inquired about the policy since her father passed away?"

Skoba nodded. "She came in just yesterday morning—she presented the required papers, and filed a claim. We informed her she should receive the policy benefit in about two weeks."

This was much as he suspected, right in line, unfortunately—she was impatient, who had seldom shown impatience before. As Ojo departed the insurance office, he noticed that across the street, beside auto parts store, stood a small mud hut—it was somebody's home, crunched in on the small lot on the corner.

Ojo returned to the Ministry dark in spirit—his worst fears seemed to be realized, and doubts he never wanted to have seemed to be amassing and hemming him in. He could still be wrong, but that likelihood was getting thinner, like a web too long buffeted in the wind, and dissipating.

When he returned to his office, Janan was waiting at his door. "Ojo, the police have found the weapon that they think killed Nagu Alema," she told him.

Seven.

Ojo and Janan arrived half an hour later at the Homicide Division, and greeted by Jeilu and Assafa at their desks; Jeilu held up a bag containing a small, average cutting knife. "This was found in the thatching of the *gocho* nearest Ngbato's house," Jeilu told them. "The hut is used for storing oil jars, barrels of grain, and sundry other supplies—this morning one of the villagers braced herself against the thatching, and the knife was dislodged."

"It's not the bejeweled ceremonial dagger I hoped we'd find," Assafa said to Janan, "but it will have to do."

"I suppose so," she mumbled, disappointed.

"That gocho is right across from Otah Mgbato's house—that seems final to me," Jeilu said.

"And, you're testing for trace," Ojo asked, referring to physical evidence on the knife.

"It's completely clean," Jeilu said. "There is no blood, hair, fibers—the lab will scan for DNA, but those results will take several days."

Ojo paused. "No blood evidence at all?

That's odd...the stab wounds were deep enough to kill Alemu."

Assafa shrugged. "He cleaned the knife before the police arrived."

"He cleaned the knife, then hid it in the thatching...very well; send it on to the lab."

Jeilu could sense something was amiss. "This should make your case, Mr. Teferra—but, you don't think so."

Ojo looked closer at the knife. "If the police arrived ten minutes after Mrs. Alemu's call, it means Mgbato had about forty minutes to kill Alemu, return to his own house, thoroughly cleanse the knife, hide it in the hut, return home, and dispose of any bloodstained clothing before those police arrived at his door."

"Doable, but, not easy," Janan said; as she did leaned a bit too far forward, and noticed Assafa's appreciation of her. "We're investigating a murder case, not speed-dating," she warned.

Assafa grinned. "Whatever could you mean?"

"He can't help it," Jeilu said, "Some men just can't handle a pretty girl, however much they might want to."

"Gentlemen, I hate to bring up the crime we're investigating; however,..."

"If it was premeditated, he could have had cleaning solutions already in place," Jeilu said.

"Why didn't he just bury the knife in the ground?"

"He couldn't, Ms. Takelo—that ground in early summer is baked stone hard, with only a thin layer of topsoil over it."

"Ngbato sees Mrs. Alemu leave the house, he knows Mr. Alemu is alone, he takes the opportunity," Assafa argued. "It sounds straightforward to me."

Ojo smiled kindly, but wasn't budging.

"We'll need the cleaning solutions he used on the knife," he told them. "The jury will need to see everything."

"In that case, we'll return to the Tahaku village—I'm betting he used vinegar."

"No; hydrogen peroxide," Assafa guessed.

"That will clean anything."

"It is possible that he planned the killing beforehand, then waited, perhaps even unconsciously, for a time to strike."

Janan didn't seem to agree. "He's nineteen—our theory rests on an impulse act, does it not?

If this is both premeditated and spontaneous, why would he not construct a better alibi?"

Ojo concurred. "His history suggests someone quick-tempered, not quick-thinking; but then, we only ever draw thumbnail sketches of people, don't we?"

"All we can do is run with the knowledge we have," Jeilu said.

Janan added, "And, what does *that* say?"

On the return drive to the Ministry building, Ojo voiced his misgivings. "I can hear Seboka now, telling the jury how Ngbato kept his sink filled with hydrogen peroxide, in case he noticed when Alemu was home alone...Ngbato is nineteen, he's just committed a murder—does he have the presence of mind to obliterate all trace evidence from his weapon, then hide it somewhere he had to have known it must be found eventually?"

"The evidence cuts both ways," Janan punned. "If he did premeditate the murder, that knife should never have been found; so, why was it?"

"And if he didn't, why carry a knife to Alemu's home?"

"Maybe the knife belonged in the Alemu home."

"Mrs. Alemu didn't report one missing, and given how her husband died, you would think she would have noticed." Ojo paused, as they merged into the dense traffic on the highway.

"Even the house of the tribal healer would have only so many utensils, especially in a poor village such as that."

Janan agreed. "What do you suppose, then?"

"Has anyone looked into the Alemu marriage?"

"Ojo, the Tahaku won't like state authorities questioning the marriage of their tribal healer," she cautioned. "The healer is a privileged position, perhaps second only to the chief."

"We could try being discreet."

She shook her head. "Inquiries won't stay discreet, not in a smallish tribe; and if we ask the wrong questions the chief is bound to object directly to the minister."

"It would be worse if we fail to follow a legitimate line of inquiry," Ojo replied. "There are unanswered questions in this case, and we cannot let that stand."

The same was true, Ojo believed, regarding the death of Kashka Selassie. The following day Ojo visited St. Mary's Hospital to speak with Kashka's physician, having first arranged a time to speak with him. Dr. Phillipe Cormenin was white, born in Marseilles, and had lived in Africa for nearly thirty years, the first ten in Nigeria. "I understand you wish to inquire about Kashka Selassie's passing," he said in English. "I'm not sure why, as Mr. Selassie died of natural causes."

"I'm interested in the particulars of his passing," Ojo told him. "What caused his arhythmia?"

"I'm not certain how much I can tell you, as doctor-patient privilege extends to one's death."

Somewhat pointedly, Ojo showed Dr.

Cormenin his prosecutor's ID. "I'm also Mr. Selassie's son-in-law," he added.

Dr. Cormenin seemed unimpressed, but accessed the file anyway. "Mr. Selassie had an elevated amount of triglycerin in his system, he was prescribed trigycerin for his heart condition, one pill per day—he evidently forgot, and took two pills the day of his death; He should have had twenty-one in his pill vial, and only twenty were remained."

"Would this overdose have been fatal?"

"Not in and of itself, but it would have put him at great risk—almost any agitation or excitement could have triggered the arhythmia."

"Did you report this overdose to any civil authorities?"

"Why," he shrugged. "Mr. Selassie was 74 years old, and lived alone—elderly people forget medications and misread dosages all the time; and not just the elderly, by the way."

"How long had he been on triglycerin?"

"Over a year—his heart condition was becoming more severe, and prior to the last three months he was prescribed a lower dosage."

Ojo was quiet a moment, then asked, "Do you know if Kashka had ever mistakenly overdosed in the past?"

"I do not know—however, I might not have been made aware of it, as his previous prescription was not so strong a dosage; therefore, such a mistake would not have put him at a high risk."

"I see...thank you."

"Is there some question to his manner of death," Dr. Cormenin asked, as Ojo was leaving. "Is there something more I should know?"

"I don't think so," Ojo said.

"And I'm to assume you would say if there was?"

"This inquiry is unlikely to involve you," Ojo said, "there is no need for suspicion on your part."

That wasn't quite good enough. "On whose part, then?"

"On mine," Ojo said, and left it at that.

From there Ojo returned to Tahaku Village to speak with Apala Nogu, Kaji Alemu's friend and fellow textile-seller, who was with Kaji was her husband was killed. In the mid-afternoon heat there was much activity throughout the village, and while most people were wearing modern clothing, some still opted for traditional dress—including two women who passed near Ojo balancing water jugs on their heads, and gave the impression that the last two hundred years had never happened.

Apala was home when Ojo arrived, and though she lived very modestly in an old shanty still offered her guest ice tea and injera. "Oh, I have known Kaji and Nega for maybe twenty years," she said warmly. "She and I were fast friends, we have always been so."

"So, you were also friends with Nega," Ojo supposed.

"We were—friendly," she said; but her tone changed, and her demeanor a little less light.

"It seems, you were not as close with Negu," he observed. "Still, as the tribal healer he was an important man."

She thought about her reply; as she started to speak a passing goat bleated outside. "He could have been a better man," Apala finally said.

"Oh? In what way?"

"Some think, he could have been a better doctor," she told him. "And he was very friendly with some in our village, with some more than others…"

"How, friendly?"

Apala sighed. "Some of the older girls and younger women of our village, he would treat for free—and, not only that…"

Ojo sighed then, too. "I understand."

"I many times told Kaji she should leave him, that Nega was not a good man; and each time she would remind me that he is the tribal healer, and in our tribe second only to the chief…so, she stayed."

"Kaji visited with you on the day Nega died?"

She said she did. "How did she seem?"

"She was angry over some patterns, some designs that she thought I'd copied from her own designs—but we talked it out, we always do; and when she left here, she said she was sorry for the harsh words, and offered to give me a new ceramic bowl."

"Then, she was in good spirits when she left?"

"I would say so."

Was she unsure? "Apala, you've known Kaji for nearly twenty years…"

"I have; and, she is hard to read." She offered more tea, and smiled. "Kaji can be very sweet, and very generous—but my friend, she is quick to temper, and she can be volatile—with her, one walks on water *and* walks on eggshells, as they say."

Ojo paused. "How has she been since Nega died?"

Apela was not naive; she saw where this question might lead. "Everyone here has noticed that Kaji is spending more time with our chief—and yet, in this time of loss, and of grief, it might be natural that she spend more time with the chief of the tribe…I will not speak against her."

"I'm not asking—"

"I am her friend; I will *not* speak against her," Apela repeated, but clearly feared she may have done just that.

Eight.

That evening it rained; not much, but so surprising was even this short period of rain that many in Abbis Ababa walked out to luxuriate in it, some children running out into the still-busy streets and getting soaked. It made the slow, congested drive home even more problematic for commuters, as they quickly switched to 'rainy season' mode, and it made the lead story on the evening news, where the anchors called it a positive omen.

Ojo noticed that Afia was still avoiding her own laptop in the evenings, and knew she'd noticed his noticing. "I'm trying to cleanse myself of bad habits," she explained; then said, "It's hard to change your behavior."

It is, he agreed. "We've found the murder weapon in the Alemu case," he mentioned. "The knife was found in one of the village gochos."

"After all this time?" She looked perplexed.

"Why didn't the killer get rid of it?"

"If Ngbato is the killer, he might not have had time," Ojo said. "But if someone else is, they might hope the knife would incriminate Ngbato."

"How hard is it to be rid of a knife?"

He gently touched her hair. "You would make a good prosecutor," he told her.

"You already do," she said, and sneaked in a quick kiss. "Your next question is, could the doer be certain the knife was found in time to implicate Ngbato, and keep free of suspicion himself?"

"That's far less certain," he admitted. "The very fact that such a common weapon was found raises its own questions—if the killer is Mgbato, and if he indeed had over 15 minutes to be rid of the evidence."

"You must also think like a defense attorney," Afia advised. "Oh, it gets tricky!"

As they touched, Ojo told her he loved her, and she said the same; he believed her, but then he always did...he had suspicions, he had nothing; he could let his suspicions go and make an end of it. Whatever he might learn, or uncover, Kashka

Selassie was dead, it made no difference to him—anything Ojo might discover could only hurt the living, and the loved.

The next afternoon he stopped by Janan's office, and invited her to lunch. "What's the occasion," she asked.

"I just want to spend time with you, away from the work trappings," Ojo said.

She smiled. "Are you asking me on a date?"

"I'm asking you out to lunch," he said again.

"Which is asking me out on a date," she keenly observed.

"I need to talk to you," he told her.

She now knew, it wasn't a date. "I'm writing an opening statement," she said. "I'll be ready by about 12:30."

As invitee Janan chose the restaurant, and picked Masafents, one of the few relatively close to the Ministry building, down Adwa Street; its classic cuisine included chicken, lamb and camel, and its clientele typically included other lawyers, judges and public officials. There were only two tables available when Janan and Ojo arrived, and curiously one of them was among the best in the dining area.

Once they'd ordered, Janan addressed the Alemu case. "Detective Panolo called this morning—there was no hydrogen peroxide in Otah Mgbato's house, and there was a new bottle of vinegar, still capped; that doesn't mean he hadn't emptied an older bottle to obliterate evidence on his knife. It's circumstantial, nothing definitive can be proven by an absence."

"If it is evidence, evidence of what—that he intended to clean in future?"

"Even a timely receipt would prove nothing, that could be a total coincidence."

"What if, for Otah Mgbato as a suspect, we substitute Kaji Alemu," Ojo pitched. "She returns home from meeting with Apala Nogo, quarrels with her husband, murders him, stashes the knife somewhere, disposes of any bloodstained clothing, then calls the police and reports finding the body."

"What is her motive?"

"According to Apala Nego, Alemu may have been cheating with other Tahaku women; also, Kaji may have been involved with the tribal chief."

"'May have been'…?"

"Motive is not an evidentiary element," Ojo said.

"And most juries will dismiss your case without it," Janan countered. "In your version, Kaji has had all this time to sanitize the knife—so if you're right, we'll learn nothing from it."

Their server presented the wine for the meal, then left. "There may be another way to test our theory," he mused. "If Kaji is guilty, and if her motives have existed for awhile, it's also possible she may not have acted alone."

"'*May* not have…'?" she echoed, again. "Unlikely; the fewer people in on your killing, the better. It's more likely she may have roped in an accessory after the fact."

Ojo fell silent for several moments. "Janan, I had another reason for needing to talk with you."

Janan first thought to insert a joke, but his tone stopped her. "What is it, Ojo?"

He thought about how to say this, there was no easy way. "Afia's father Kashka passed away recently, as you know; and, the Medical Examiner has determined he died of natural causes, and has closed the case…I think that decision might be premature."

"You think, it's something else?"

He thought before speaking, he clearly questioned whether he should. "There are elements concerning his passing that raise questions, questions I would hesitate to raise."

"Do you think you should open an investigation?"

He tensed. "Janan, I think Afia might be involved."

"Oh, my God…your *wife*?" Instinctively, she placed her hand on his. "Why?"

Ojo laid out the reasons for his suspicions, and how he came to his conclusions—it was circumstantial, he was quick to admit, some of it even subjective; still, it was not one thing, but many, and most of his suspicions arose from Ojo knowing Afia better than almost anyone, aside from her father. And curiously, his suspicions were so strong, because her behavior was *so* foreign to the Afia he'd always known. "Life changes people; time, experience, grief changes people, I know that—and I know, this is not like that."

When their lunches arrived they barely seemed to notice, aside from giving thanks.

"When you say 'involved'," Janan carefully clarified, "you do mean, responsible…?"

"I mean, I think she killed him," Ojo said.

The starkness of his sentence startled Janan, who quickly looked away. "Then, you believe your wife is capable of murder—and don't remind me that we'll all capable of killing; this is different from that."

"Afia is very smart," he told her. "I think she decided on what she saw as a logical course of action, given her father's age, his condition, his limited future, and her motive."

"Murder, as a risk-benefit analysis…"

"I think she could justify killing him, if her plan proved successful," Ojo said. As he spoke he glanced round him, to be certain no-one else could hear him. "Afia isn't very religious, but she isn't amoral—she's capable of creating a construct where such an action is viable."

"But her husband is a precinct prosecutor," Janan objected, logically enough. "How could she possibly evade suspicion?"

He paused. "Perhaps she did expect it, and gambled on whether I'd act on my suspicions…

and perhaps, I'm totally wrong. There may be other explanations. I have become so jaded in this position over the last ten years, I'm seeing any aberrations as signs of evil."

Janan at last turned to her food, not knowing what to say next. "If you accuse her, your marriage will be over," she quietly told him. "And if you open an investigation, and you're wrong, you also risk destroying your career.

You could lose everything."

"And if I don't, and she is guilty...I have no proof, Janan; no tangible, solid piece of evidence.

I still can't be certain Kashka didn't overdose by accident."

She motioned that he should eat, which he finally started. "You said yourself, people change...you could simply let this play out as is, and observe her behavior, and determine some way of proceeding over time. Justice need not be swift in every case," she said; then added, "There are no statutory limits on murder."

"That could make me tantamount to an accomplice, especially if I benefit from no investigation being mounted—I'm not just an involved party, Janan, I'm an officer of the court."

"Screw 'officer of the court'—you're talking about the woman you love!"

"We cannot obey the canon of ethics only when it's convenient," he proposed, none-too-forcefully, "nor is this a minor crime."

"*If* it's a crime, if she's guilty," she pressed. "All you have is a series of behaviors that could be explained in other ways. But once you start an investigation, there's no going back."

"If I establish what I would otherwise accept as proof, and still do nothing,—"

"It means, you're human! If I thought a member of my family was guilty of something terrible, I would still want to defend them."

"'Not bear the knife myself'*," he quoted.

**Macbeth.*

"The impetus is still yours," Janan reasoned, and as if for emphasis then messed with her chicken salad. "No jury would convict on a charge of accomplice."

"That's not the point." This time, Ojo took her free hand in his. "I don't know what to do."

She held his hand. "You will, Ojo—I believe in you; and, I believe you'll see what's right to do."

"How can I know," he quietly said, looking away to the busy bustle outside, staring away into nothing.

Nine.

On Saturday morning Ojo and Afia visited the National Museum, which displayed priceless artifacts from all throughout the history of Ethiopia. The couple had toured the museum before, of course, but Ojo requested they return, claiming such visits was calming to him, and he was feeling much pressure related to the upcoming Ngbato trial—nor was Afia simply tagging along, as her interest in history was in fact keener than his, and her knowledge more inclusive.

Ojo wore a light-blue shirt, tan jeans and tennis shoes, which could have given the impression he was employed there—she, however, in a loose yellow blouse and formfitting white slacks, looked like a film star (all Afia's look lacked was her sunglasses tucked into her blouse, whereas hers dangled from her pocket).

There was no good historical plan to the museum exhibits, or its temporal progression, as the wing housing items from the 19th-Century Italian occupation stood beside relics from the Solomonic reigns, and the same floor that included the Islamic influences from the 600s and items from the reign of Melilick II, whose Ethiopian rule began in 1889. Each floor was decorated in the red, white and green of the national flag, and this lent some sense of place, if not necessarily continuity.

Ojo and Afia began their walk-through from the third floor, starting at the top, the same way one washes a horse—many displays they simply noticed and walked by, ancient blankets, old sandals and such, til Afia stopped at an exhibit of jewelry once owned by Emperor John IV from the 19th Century. They were necklaces, rings and cuffs of gold-and-silver inlay, some with set with emeralds and rubies. "Imagine how poor the typical family was then," Afia said sadly, "and, most still are."

"It wasn't just ostentation," Ojo said. "This was a display of power."

"Of dominion," she agreed, and they walked on. "Even then rulers thought nothing of using superstition and intimidation to control their subjects, even under a Christian rubric."

"Was Constantine inspired, or deluded," Ojo mused. "By one view he was a reformer; by the other, an apostate."

"Not every belief must be accepted as legitimate," she posited. "There must be some semblance of relevance."

"Isn't that inherent by the very nature of belief?"

"If so, then false prophets are still prophets," she said.

"Even prophets require credential," Ojo said.

"One cannot just sound off, and expect to be followed; even Mohammed—"

That caught her interest. "What about Mohammed?"

"He was already a leader before his enlightenment."

"Even Jesus was a rabbi, and so an authority figure…what about Buddha?"

Ojo grinned. "What about Buddha?"

He was not a prophet," she affirmed with a tiny triumph in her voice. "So, your prophet theory dissolves."

Just a ways on were precious finds from the Aksumite kingdom, the diverse and loosely-allied tribes that dominated the region for over 800 years soon after the time of Christ. On display were headdresses, weapons and musical instruments, and near the end of the hall a black mannequin dressed in a chieftain's ceremonial robes; in the glass case before him were ancient knives, and a brightly-painted spear.

They were quiet a moment before the figure, when Afia spoke softly. "I should confess, I lied to you," she said, turning Ojo's way. "I saw my father on the night he passed away."

He looked surprised, because he was. "You did?"

She sighed, as if sharing this was of no real consequence. "Inaya and I left the film early because I was feeling ill," she explained, and gestured to continue walking. "but soon after we separated I felt better, and on the way home I decided on an impulse to visit my father, since I hadn't seen him in a couple of weeks, as he had been feeling poorly. I thought it might do Kashka good, maybe because I was just feeling poorly myself, and worked through it. There was no more to it than that."

She and Ojo were now walking downstairs to the second floor, that centered on the Solomonic line, and also included a collection from the rule of Empress Zauditu. "It's a very late visit," Ojo mentioned, "It must have come as quite a surprise to your father."

"It wasn't a good idea," she admitted. "Once I arrived I thought better of it, but I was already there, so...So, we spoke briefly in his den—we were conspiring, I must admit—but it did not go well, and he was somewhat upset when I left."

"You were conspiring?"

She smiled a little shyly. "He was pushing for grandchildren," Afia said. "He was worried about his health, and he was fretting because you and I hadn't yet started a family. That's why he wanted to talk to me, to in effect pressure me to have a child soon, 'by next Spring', he hoped.

I think he was afraid he may not live to see his first grandchild."

"Why didn't you tell me this before?"

"I was being secretive about it for no reason, really, except wanting to surprise you; a child is a gift from God, you see…it seems foolish now."

"Not at all," he non-committed, now that she had. "I certainly don't need to know everything about your relationship…how long did you stay?"

"At my father's house?" They stopped briefly at an exhibit dedicated to Prince Almaq, who increased Muslim rule in the 13th Century; the display included old documents, clothing from the time, and little trinkets like pearled earrings and gold bracelets. "Oh, about fifteen minutes, no more than half an hour, I think—when I came home I just wanted to head off to bed."

She had preempted him. She could now account for her presence at Kashka's house that evening, should an investigation begin, and security footage from the home reveal her there.

And the story about Kashka wanting grandchildren was plausible—he had mentioned it before; and, he was someone accustomed to influencing others by incentive. If this was an admirable dodge, if in fact that's what it was.

"You said nothing about feeling ill the next morning," Ojo lightly said, trying to sound neutral, or only mildly concerned.

"Why would I? I actually felt all right by the time I had reached Kashka's house." Her lips moved, almost but not quite into a smile. "It's odd, that I still don't say 'my father's house'—that's a holdover from childhood. When I was a little girl, the Christian schools referred to Heaven as 'our Father's house', and I still carry that phrase in me somewhere, even after all these years...isn't that odd?"

When they continued on they stopped to admire the display honoring Empress Zauditu, and her entry into the League of Nations in 1923.

Afia had long been interested in the empress; her essay on this controversial figure had been printed several years back in *Abbis Admas*. "You were reading her biography recently," Ojo noted.

"Observant of you," Afia said. "She was ahead of her time—she had an unique vision of the future for Ethiopia." She paused. "But, events overtook her. She had much with which she had to contend, and the past conspired to stop her."

"Not only the past," he remarked.

"Zauditu's decisions were sound, but she trusted the wrong people; and in that society lacked the resources to seek the proper redress," Afia said. "In the end, it was her faith that let her down."

"Was it," Ojo said; half question, half affirmation—and whether Afia meant her faith in people around her, or her faith in God, she never made clear.

On the ground floor stood the most famous and unique exhibit of the National Museum, that devoted to the skeleton discovered by a lake in Afar, the *Australopithecus afarensis* globally known as 'Lucy'. The exhibit took pride of place on the ground floor, being an arboreal scene with a model of Lucy as she might have looked, perched alert and watchful up in the branches of a tree; and in a glass case her skull and several bones were displayed, along with text devoted to the find, her age, probable lifestyle, and even how she likely met her end.

Afia marveled at the exhibit, even though she'd seen it more than once. "These aren't her actual bones," she told her husband, as though he didn't know this already. "The sections that resemble bone around the plaster casting are a polymer mix—her actual bones are safely secured in the museum vaults."

"Dinquinesh is still amazing," Ojo said.

Dinquinesh is Lucy's Ethiopian name.

"Later anthropologists have found earlier ancestors of *Astralopithecus,* one dating over a half-million years earlier—but she is still our star, she always will be." Afia stood admiring the display, which was excellently-done; so well-done, one could see no obvious link between her and later homo sapiens.

"Lucy did popularize the *Astrals*; and of course, she has the added allure of having been named for a Beatles' song."

"Luckily, those anthropologists that found her weren't listening to 'Louie Louie'."

"This says, scientists believe she fell from a tree," Ojo noted. "I don't believe it."

"Neither do I—she knew what she was doing, why would she have fallen?" She smiled, and gave a sneaky look. "I suspect foul play..."

Ten.

Monday morning started with bad news from Janan's office. "The forensics lab has examined the knife found near Ngbato's house," Janan said, said report in hand. "There is no trace of DNA anywhere on it—not on the blade, the handle... nothing."

He took the report from her, incredulous. "How is that possible?"

"A very thorough cleaning would do it—and Ngbato did have time to do it, though only just."

Ojo looked incredulous. "This 19-year-old hothead manages to cover his tracks this well?

I don't believe it."

"It does speak to premeditation," Janan said, "down to buying a new bottle of vinegar; and, it is more likely that Tahaku would use a more organic cleaning agent, such as vinegar, as opposed to hydrogen peroxide."

"And, yet..." As he stared at the forensics report, Ojo raised his eyebrows. "Janan, what if we're searching in the wrong place?"

"How so?"

"Magicians use misdirection—maybe we should, too. How does your calendar look this morning? Are you up for a trip to the Tahaku village?"

"We need to prep for pretrial motions," she reminded him. "The hearing is tomorrow."

He acknowledged this, but was undeterred.

"We need two lab techs to accompany us, as well as detectives Panolo and Kamada, and we'll need them for the shank of the morning, if not the afternoon. If I'm right, Janan, we'll need to seriously amend our motion to the court."

The officers took three state cars to the village that morning, which garnered a good deal of attention—the usually-busy villagers watched with growing curiosity, as Ojo and Janan headed for the opulent home of the Tahaku chief, and the detectives and technicians made for the gocho nearest the Ngbato house, the hut where the murder weapon was found.

Chief Nissanke was a tallish, middle-aged man of surety and self-possession, partly gray-haired, smooth-faced, and square-built; he wore an expensive Italian suit, and a traditional Tahaku necklace inset with amethyst and lapis lapuli as a symbol of office. He had been called that morning to expect the prosecutors, and had coffees and biscuits readied on silver trays.

"Your office had not yet afforded me the privilege of an official visit," he complained while smiling.

"You detained a member of my tribe without so much as a single word to my office—I might have expected better, Mr. Teferra."

"I did plan to call you before trial, Chief Nissanke," Ojo told him.

"This charming flower would me Ms.

Takelo," he said, and offered his hand. "You are most welcome in my house."

"I'm more of a Venus Flytrap," she claimed with a grin. "Thank you for seeing us."

He gestured to the coffees and biscuits. "Please, partake; I find the summers so long and so wearying, I tend to overeat through them, to my detriment...please sit, and tell me how I can help you in this sad and disturbing matter."

Ojo leaned forward. "As you know, federal law supersedes tribal law in Ethiopia, and that any investigation into capital crimes has the right to enter tribal lands, and conduct a legal search pursuant to a judicial warrant..." He then gave the warrant to Chief Nissanke. "This gives us the right to search any communal property on or adjacent to Tahaku land."

Nissanke read the warrant and said, "Yes, this looks to be in order."

"And as you know, we currently hold Otah Ngbato in custody under suspicion of killing your tribal healer, Nega Alemu."

"Oh, but I am certain he is innocent," the chief said. "I know young Otah, and he is a good person."

"Do you suspect someone else of the crime," Janan asked. "His wife Kaji, for example?"

"No, no; I wouldn't think she could have done it, either—Kaji is also a good person."

"What about the 90-year-old Juba Toko, who's bedridden—could she have done it?"

"Of course not," he asserted. "I have known Juba for decades, and she too is a good person!"

"Oh; I see," Ojo said. "So, pretty much anyone who is Tahaku is a good person?" Nissanke grinned.

"Did anyone from outside the tribe visit the village on the day Alemu was killed?"

"Not that I know," the chief told them.

"Then, what do you suppose must have happened?"

"That is your work to determine—mine, is to ensure the safety and prosperity of my people."

He poured himself another coffee. "*I* did not kill Nega, and I know of no-one who I think capable of having done so. I look forward to your release of Otah Ngbato, and to our simple village life returning to normal."

"Chief Nissanke, we will follow this investigation to wherever the evidence leads," Ojo told him, "even if the evidence leads us right back here."

"I have nothing to hide—however, I will not be harassed; I will not hesitate to speak with Chief Prosecutor Zenawi, if I must."

"We feel the same," Janan said.

He sipped his coffee. "Is there anything else?"

Ojo set down his coffee. "There is—would you be good enough to point out to us where you store your essential oil jars and grain barrels?"

He paused, a bit surprised. "There are two gochos that hold our kegs and barrels; one is near—"

"Would you please step outside, and show us," Janan asked kindly. "We don't want to make any mistakes."

Nissanke seemed wary, but did as requested, and from his front door stairs pointed to the two gochos; beside the one nearer the Ngbato house stood the ministry investigators and technicians, the latter carrying test kits. "I see your people are skilled in guesswork," he snipped.

More to the point, many of the villagers were watching the chief speaking with the prosecutors and pointing to the gochos, including Nega Alemu's widow Kaji.

"Thank you very much, Chief Nissanke," Ojo said, and shook his hand. "Our office will keep a closer contact with yours in future."

Nissanke smiled, and carefully kept his gaze far from Kaji Alemu's direction. "Thank you, and may you two have a safe and pleasant journey back to the city."

As Ojo and Janan walked down the central village road, they noticed Kaji Alemu was still watching them; once noticed, she started to enter her house, but a step or two too late.

"May we speak with you a moment, Mrs. Alemu?" Ojo approached her, and motioned to Janan. "This is my colleague, Assistant Prosecutor Janan Takelo."

"Pleased to meet you…won't you come in?"

Taji sat on her couch, as her guests took chairs facing her. "I saw you just now, speaking with Chief Nissanke; I assume you talked about Otah Ngbato's case, yes?"

"His trial date will be put on calendar tomorrow," Janan told her.

"We still have a couple of questions regarding Ngbato," Ojo admitted. "You may be able to help clarify matters."

"If you think I could, of course," Kaji said.

The knife used in the murder of your husband was found in the storage gocho near Ngbato's home…do you know who found it?"

She said yes. "Kafi discovered it—Kafi Madhin, who's one of our neighbors; she was taking some cooking oil. She brought the knife to Chief Nissanke."

"We're tested the knife in our forensic lab in Addis Ababa, and found no evidence on it—no fingerprints, no DNA; the knife is absolutely clean."

"Ngbato must have wiped the knife clean," Kaji said.

"He couldn't have simply wiped it clean," Janan told her. "That wouldn't work, there would still be traces remaining."

Kaji glanced in the direction of the storage gocho, though of course she couldn't see it where she was. "Is that why your scientists are there searching, to collect other evidence he might have left behind?"

"We don't expect to find any," Janan said.

"And we should," Ojo added. "Your husband's murder occurred during the heat wave that started at the beginning of summer, and the gocho is constructed of living materials, saplings and thatched grasses—these materials readily absorb and retain contact trace DNA. Ngbato had to come in significant contact with the thatching, when he hid the knife."

"In the midday heat, Otah Ngbato's perspiration would be retained by the gocho, and place him there like a photograph," Janan said.

Kaji hesitated. "What if we wore gloves?"

"Ngbato doesn't own any gloves," Janan told her.

"He was here, he might have stolen gloves from the house."

"No—Ngbato has larger hands than your husband's, and far larger than yours."

Kaji took a breath. "Then someone must have lent him gloves," she quickly said.

"Who—and, why? Our detectives are asking his friends and neighbors, but so far no-one has admitted lending Otah Ngbato any gloves."

"If our lab technicians find no trace of Otah Ngbato in the interior thatching, we will need to expand our search for another viable suspect—one who had the motive and the opportunity to kill your husband."

"He was not always a good man, he—"

"We know this, Mrs. Alemu; we know you knew about his affairs with other Tahaku women.

We also know, that you've been seeing Chief Nissanke."

"And you own gloves, Mrs. Alemu," Janan said. "You just intimated as much."

Kaji was still for a moment; then, "I should say nothing more now—I think, I would like to consult with a solicitor."

"That may be best for you," Ojo agreed. "Would you agree to accompany our detectives into the city?"

"Would I follow them?"

"I think it best, that you ride with them."

When detectives Panolo and Kamada came to the Alemu house, Chief Nissanke was with them. "I myself will arrange for your attorney, Kaji—say nothing to the authorities until you've spoken with him. I will see you again shortly."

"As you say..." She glanced back to her house. "When you search the house, please be very careful with the family photographs—many are very old and fragile, and some are not put into albums. I don't want them damaged."

"Of course," Janan assured her. "We'll be certain that every precaution is taken."

Once Kaji was driven away, Nissanke turned to the prosecutors. "I do not believe it of Kaji," he said; then, "The way you keep arresting my people, I'm starting to think you intend to empty out my village."

"We hope this is the last," Kanan told him.

The chief watched the detectives' car disappear in the distance. "I will speak with Uba Zenawi as to which firm should defend Kaji…have either of you a recommendation?"

"We are in effect her opposition," Ojo reminded him. "We may not be the best people to ask."

"You are district officers who would address the question honestly," Nissanke replied. "Your work is to find the truth by whatever means, is it not?"

"It is," Ojo said, trying to read Nissanke, and wondering if he ever could.

Eleven.

On the morning following Senoir Prosecutor Zenawi received a call from Chief Nissanke, who asked to meet; they chose *Palais du Diamont*, one of the most upscale restaurants in all of Addis Ababa. Once they were seated, Chief Nissanke started in. "I trust of course that you can appreciate the delicacy of my position," the chief said, "as I must concern myself with both the potential danger to Mrs. Alemu, and the welfare of the Tahaku in general."

"I appreciate your potential involvement," replied Zenawi. "As you were Alemu's lover, you two share mutual motives."

"Only in a speculative senss; I have partnered with other Tahaku, Mr. Zenawi, and I assure you, their husbands are all still alive—well, all but one, and he had a bad heart, you can ask anyone."

They ordered their meals in French, as that's what was done there; then Zenawi focused their talk more specifically. "What is it you want, Chief Nissanke?"

"I am hoping the good name of the Tahaku come through this sad sequence of events with as little damage as possible; and to that end, that I as tribal leader be kept in the periphery to the farthest extent possible."

Zenawi sipped his lemon water, then said, "How might that be? You provide the catalyst, you are material to this case in every sense."

"But I have no direct involvement, nor indirect involvement—it is not certain yet that I was even a catalyst; no; just as I want the Tahaku involvement downplayed, I expect that my own purely tangential connection minimized, as well."

Zenawi sighed. "It is not up to me, chief; it'a matter for all the Office of Prosecution. Have you spoken with Junior Prosecutor Teferra?"

"He was not coop—that is, he was not particularly helpful; he spoke in careful terms, which must be expected from a junior."

"I see..." Their orders arrived, but neither man seemed much in food. "Then, let me speak in less careful terms—there are many avenues of influence and obstruction in cases like Mrs. Alemu's case; and, my office will penalize anyone who uses such tactics...*anyone*, Chief Nissanke."

"We both want the best outcome possible."

Zenawi smiled. "I must admit, I'm curious as to why you haven't yet spoken out concerning the arrest of Mr. Mgbatu?"

"I had planned to," said the chief. "I thought I would speak after his pretrial hearing; but I say again, I will strongly oppose any unnecessary intrusion into Tahaku tribal affairs."

Once he phrased it that way, he thought better of it.

Zenawi couldn't resist. "I'm afraid, it's your tribal affairs that started all this."

At the pretrial hearing the following day, prosecutors requested a writ of release for Otah Ngbato, to the surprise of the *arawja* court. "You had sufficient evidence to indict," said Judge Kasada. "Am I to take it, then, that said evidence is insufficient for trial?"

"New evidence has come to light which argues against Mr. Mgbato's involvement," Ojo explained. "The state therefore withdraws its charges."

"Indeed?" Kasada nodded, but seemed skeptical. "Have you someone else in mind for this most heinous crime?"

"We do."

The judge looked relieved. "An, have you secured an indictment against this individual?"

"We have; and moreover, we are prepared to proceed against her."

Kasada glanced to his docket. "That would be the victim's wife, Taji Alemu—is she present at present?"

She was, as her counsel Mohammed Seboka confirmed. "The defense requests ROR, as my client has never been arrested, and never so much as issued a parking ticket."

"The defendant doesn't have a driving license," Janon pointed out.

"She is a respected member of the Tahaku tribe—they own very few cars."

Kasada smiled, but not with warmth. "You cannot expect a release on recognizance when your client is accused of murder, Mr. Seboka, nor shall be a bill be brought for consideration; your client is remanded…as for the state's release writ for Mr. Mgbato, let's not hold too many people for this one crime, your writ is granted. Now, if there's nothing else,—"

"Your Honor, we intend to file a request for change of venue, to Dire Dawa."

"Why? Are they nicer to murderers in Dire Dawa?"

"There has been much local press coverage on this case, most of it negative to my client."

"Your Honor, we have read the newspaper accounts of this crime, and Mrs. Alemu was simply named as the accused."

"I'd call that negative," Seboka said.

"We have also seen local news broadcasts that carried this story," Janan added. "None of them have reported any further than the State's press release."

"Which itself stands against my client."

"The State opposes a change of venue, as a costly and unnecessary waste of time."

"That's all right with me," Kaji said.

Judge Kasada thought it over, which didn't take long. "I think we can find a jury that's not vengeful and bloodthirsty, right here in Addis Ababa," he ruled. "Motion denied; we set a trial date is set for three weeks from today."

Chief Nissanke then stood. "Your Honor, I respectfully request this matter be reassigned to the Council of Tribal Justice."

"Defense counsel already brought this motion," Kasada said. "Capitol murder is squarely set in the jurisdiction of the State, even if said offense occurred on tribal land."

"I disagree," said Nissanke, "and if necessary I will appeal to the Ministry board."

Kasada paused; then ordered, "Conference—in my chambers." So the attorneys, the defendant and Chief Nissanke followed the judge into his narrow chambers, a tight fit; the room was like a closet full of law books, only with a desk and chair. "Now then, what is the basis for your argument?"

"I contend that this may not be a capitol case, as death may have occurred by manslaughter, or even by accident."

"Accident?" Ojo reacted. "So, she held her knife out, and he repeatedly just stepped into it?"

"We could at least argue some such point."—which was perhaps not the best choice of words.

"Your Honor, the crime was committed by and to Tahaku on Tahaku soil, which is no less independent than the grounds of an embassy."

"You're now acknowledging, it was a crime."

"Hypothetically," Nissanke added—Saboka stayed quiet, as this was the first he'd heard of it.

"Your Honor, case law is quite settled on this."

"There is also a question of conflict-of interest," Janan said. "Chief Nissanke would be High Adjudicator at a Tahaku tribunal, and he is himself materially involved with this case."

"In what way?"

"His involvement is not of a criminal nature; however, it eliminates any semblance of impartiality."

"I see—well then, that motion is also denied." When the chief moved to speak once more, Kasada raised his hand. "Enough—please don't annoy this court, Chief Nissanke; it will do you no good."

That afternoon Ojo and Janan began the work of building a case against Kaju Alemu.

They had not yet spent an hour on this after the hearing, when called in to meet with Senior Prosecutor Zenawi.

"Ive already received two calls from Chief Nissanke, and one from Nissanke's counsel," Zenawi told them. "The chief is very concerned about the possible prosecution of Nega Alemu's widow."

"She has motive, means, opportunity," Janan checked off, "Add to that tampering with evidence, suspicious conduct..."

"She attempted to frame Otah Ngbato for the crime." Ojo chimed in. "It shows consciousness of guilt."

"Someone attempted to frame him, but you can't prove yet that it was Kaji Alemu; the chief was very keen to point that out to me, more than once—he also made it very clear, he does not wish to testify himself. He *promises* he has nothing germane to add." Zenawi consulted his monitor. "When is your trial date?"

"August 22."

"Do you have any way to establish who owned the murder weapon?"

"It's a common household knife," Janan told him. "and it's not new, there's probably a thousand such knives in the Tahaku village."

"And have you exhausted the possibility of someone else having committed this crime?"

Ojo shrugged. "The next most likely suspect would be Chief Nissanke himself."

"I'm sure he'd be thrilled to hear that." Zenawi thought things over for a moment, then spoke. "The chief is pressuring me to release Mrs. Alemu into his custody as tribal leader until the trial—do either of you have reason to believe he might be a co-conspirator?"

"He might be a post-offense accessory," Janan said. "We think the two are romantically involved, which goes to motive."

"So it does...I'll deny the chief's request as against federal interest; but if he appeals to the Council of Ministers, we may need to defend our custody in court."

"If Nissanke pushes this to the Supreme Court, he has an advantage—recent rulings have opposed the People's House, and favored an increase in tribal autonomy."

Zenawi nodded. "Then it's in our interest to see that Chief Nissanke never makes the appeal."

Ojo and Janan returned to his office, and considered the options. "We can't consider a manslaughter charge with the evidence we have," Janan said. "Unless she offers a provocation defense, our hands are tied."

"And it wasn't a crime of passion," Ojo mentioned. "Murder for gain is a capital offense."

"Her husband's rival was the tribal chief—why couldn't she have had an affair with the village auto mechanic?"

"That's still gain." Ojo smiled. "Is there any evidence of domestic abuse?"

"Two hospital visits—only, it was *him* going to hospital; once, with a fractured wrist. His accounts concerning how he was injured are of no help to us."

He gestured his surrender. "In that case, barring an affirmative defense, we have to hope for a confession."

"A confession? Ojo, she won't talk to us at all, she won't so much as tell us the time!"

"Then we convince her to talk to us," he suggested; only, he had no idea how they might accomplish this.

That Friday Afia received notice via email that she had been awarded the death benefit from Shewa Federal Insurance for Kasha's death, and the payout had been transferred to her account, as prearranged.

Afia was so happy at the news, that she was in overflowing good spirits all that evening—joking and teasing, she showed joy and relief in almost everything she did; she even volunteered to whip up a dessert, which was unusual for her. She cuddled with Ojo over a favorite film they hadn't seen in years—she laughed him out of patience, laughed him into patience, shared her sweet wine with him, and with bright smiles and sparkling eyes she drunk him to their bed.

Ojo woke early next morning to Afia's light kisses on his chest; she lay atop him, as she often did (as she was lighter), and greeted with a soft, quiet salutation. "It's only now after seven," she said. "We could stay we could sleep in."

"If I sleep now, I won't be up til noon," he said.

"Oh?" She nudged with her hip. "You wouldn't lie to me."

Ojo grinned. "Not about sleeping til noon..."

She hummed, and rested her head to hear his heartbeat. "I want to rake a trip, today or tomorrow—I want to visit *Tis Isat*." *Tis Isat* is the

Ethiopian name for The Blue Nile Falls, just southeast of Bahir Dar.

"I think, they're the same as last year," Ojo replied.

"No, they can't be—'never the same river twice'..." She looked at him. "Are you awake?"

She shifted a bit. "I suppose."

She took a moment. "We can't touch the money from the insurance; I'm afraid, it's already spoken for—and much of the inheritance as well, I'm afraid."

Ojo was well awake now. "Oh?"

"I have a confession to make...the reason money has been so tight recently, why I've been so preoccupied—I've been indulging in online gambling. I don't know why, maybe a reaction to stress, I don't know...but it's gone too far, and worse, I haven't been winning."

He looked concerned. "How bad is it?"

"It's bad," Afia said.

"Tell me."

"I owe over 200,000 birr," she quickly said, ripping off the bandage. "I know I should have stopped; I know, I should have told you. I couldn't see how, I couldn't see how to face you." She sighed, and braced herself. "Now, you know."

Afia's confession was worse than it would have been otherwise; it gave her motive. Ojo took a few seconds, deciding how to respond. "Does this windfall cover the debt you've incurred?"

"It has," she said. "That's why I was online for so long last night, I was covering my debts—that's done now." She glanced slightly away.

"We have perhaps 12,000 birr remaining."

Only that much, from the benefits from her father's death; hardly profit, by any standard.

Ojo sighed. "Well, as you say—it's done now."

She smiled. "You're not angry with me?"

He touched her lovely face, uncertain how much to say. "I am sorry that you've lost your benefits, but no, I'm not angry. How could I be, when it was your money."

"Then you forgive me?"

Ojo pressed her a little bit closer. "There is nothing to forgive, Afia—though now, I can forget that trip to Monaco."

"We can't even afford Morocco."

"We could always visit De Gaulle Square."

This was in downtown Addis Ababa.

But she couldn't smile; she trembled a bit, and gave a small kiss. "I am *so* sorry, Ojo; I don't know how I let it get so out-of-hand, honestly. I always thought I could rein it in, I never—"

"No, no—let be," he whispered, and held her, and wondered who he was holding.

Twelve.

Tis Isat, which means 'The Water That Smokes', is one of the most spectacular waterfalls in all the world, a 150-foot drop across a width of 1,300 feet, a cascading roar of waters that can be heard miles away. The chasm stands where the Blue Nile meets the White, and the fabulous display of mists and rainbows seen every day draw admirers from across the continent, especially after the rainy season when the Falls are at their mightiest.

Ojo and Afia drove to the falls on Sunday morning, paid the 20-birr admission fee at the ticket office, then followed the small green signs over paved walkways and rocky inclines that lead to the 'eastern route', a 40-minute uphill hike to the inset public areas that afford the best and safest viewpoints of the falls.

"I first came here when I was a little girl," Afia mentioned along the approach. "I was nine or ten, and as magnificent as the sight of *Tis Isat,* what I remember most was the sound—that terrible, endless roar, like a lioness forever warning the world away."

Ojo glanced at her. "You still remember that?"

"I've never forgotten it," Afia told him. "I've come here twice since then, last time with you—but it never made me feel the same way."

"I wanted to propose to you here," Ojo said.

"but that day I lost my nerve; maybe just as well, Since I couldn't keep your attention more than a minute while we were here."

She grinned. "You're wrong; you had my full attention all that time...I recall being nervous over a modeling assignment in Nairobi the next day, but I also suspected you had something underhanded in mind."

"Out-of-hand, as it happened," Ojo said. "When I proposed that weekend, I felt like I was making up for a missed opportunity."

"'The Accidental Proposal'—sounds like someone's novel," Afia remarked. "Be careful walking this part, it's wet and slippery..."

The enormous roaring falls tumbled endlessly ahead, creating curliques of light that shimmered through the sparkly mists; the flatland above was mostly hidden in dark dense foliage, completely still in contrast to the white rushing waters down from Lake Tana, and beyond the distant hills more an impression of contours off in the hazy distance.

After a time they had climbed to 'the Portuguese Bridge', the 17th-century walkway that spanned a rocky and shadowy crevice, and from which the falls could be partly seen—already, the roar of *Tis Isat* was increasingly loud and reverberant. Afia and Ojo stopped near the midpoint of the bridge, and admired the lush and lovely scenery. "We stopped here back then," Ojo recalled. "This is where my courage gave out."

She took his hand. "History doesn't repeat itself—that's a myth."

He turned to her. "I think you killed your father."

"I know you do."

He looked away; from where they stood, a misty rainbow could be seen over the falls; beneath the bridge the rich foliage darkened into a blackness below, and no woodland floor be seen, a darkness like that one imagined in the Poe story that featured a bottomless pit. Voices could be heard, nearby but faint, and Ojo saw another couple approaching the same way they came.

"Let's continue on," he said.

When they reached the primary viewpoint, only a few people were also present, and the incessant pounding sound of the falls made all but the briefest talk viable—instead, the couple admired the view mostly in silence, a silence that continued a few minutes after they'd started back down again to the base; so permeating was the cleansing mist from the falls, even at that distance, that the couple's clothes were wet clean through by then.

"If my father was killed," Afia finally said, "it was very well done, almost flawlessly."

"I'm glad you can appreciate its aesthetic."

"I explained to you why I was there that night, and why I lied," she said. "My fingerprints will be all over Kashka's house—as will yours, and those of any number of people."

"Will your prints be on his prescription vial?"

"If a killer tricked a victim into an overdose, that killer might wipe the vial clean, then reapply the victim's prints onto the vial…is that not possible?"

"I'm told the overdose itself might not be enough," Ojo told her. "that some other shock or agitation might have been needed."

"Maybe," Afia agreed. "Maybe the killer threatened the victim, shook him forcefully, screamed at him violently—until he finally suffered cardiac arrest…" Her voice was no longer even, but shaking. "If so, how horrible."

He helped her over a few dicey steps across moss-encircled stretches, but could not look her in the eye. "Afia, if the Ministry tries to prove—"

"There's nothing to prove," she insisted. "There is nothing for the authorities to find, nothing; he's gone, he was old, and ill, and now, he is gone…I asked that we come here for a reason. You see, Kashka got his wish, only a little too late—Ojo, I am expecting a child!"

He held her to him, smiling without thinking.

"Are you sure?"

She nodded happily. "I've tested twice, and confirmed it with my gynecologist; we're having a baby."

He was not only surprised; he was at first conflicted, which he quickly hid. "We are, are you are really certain…?"

Afia laughed. "Yes, I just told you—yes!"

Ojo kissed her lightly, and he noticed her dark hair sparkling with tiny beads of water; but, his thoughts were chaos—it was now not just her that he might act against. "How long have you known?"

"No time at all," she told him. "I found out only three days ago. And of course, we couldn't take the same boat ride again, where you finally proposed…so, I thought of this."

He looked at her sadly. "But, what I know,—"

"You don't," Afia quickly said. "Ojo, you don't *know* anything…you could let be." When he started to speak, she touched his lips to hush him.

"You could."

"How could I?"

"Just so—how could you?" She kept those dark, beautiful eyes on him. "If the baby is a boy, I want to name him Kashka."

"I understand," he said, and held her closer.

Thirteen.

On the following Tuesday Ojo entered his office to find Senior Prosecutor Zenawi waiting for him; Janan Takelo was there, as well. "Ojo, there's been a development," Zenawi told him.

"Kaji Alemu has requested a new attorney, and the Kahaku have hired Adeba Sisay, of Zadua, Wolde and Sisay—and she's requested a meeting."

Ojo was still setting down his things. When?"

"In half an hour," Janan told him. "*Tenastallan**, Ojo!" *Good morning, and good health.

The prosecutors arrived at the jail inside half an hour; Mrs. Alemu and Ms. Sisay were waiting for them in the Interrogation Room, along with Chief

Nissanke. "I am Adeba Sisay," she said, a tall, thin woman with blue-braided hair and a light, transparent scarf, "and you both know my client, and her tribal chief."

"You should be reminded, Mrs. Alemu, that your interests and those of your tribe might diverge," Ojo warned. "In that light, you might question the propriety of Chief Nissanke's presence here; he embodies a clear conflict on interest. His closeness to this case renders his involvement problematic."

"Nonsense," Nissanke dismissed. "Kaji cannot be expected to appreciate such distinctions from her tribal leader; that is why I am here." He smoothed his pricey dark suit with his hand. "I represent the Tahaku in this matter."

"And he does so with Mrs. Alemu's full consent," Sisay added, and sat beside Kaji.

"I'm not surprised," Janan remarked.

Ojo turned to Kaji, whose gaze was on Chief Nissanke. "Mrs. Alemu, you must not regard his position as completely supportive of yours—as he says, his concern is not necessarily for you."

"Ask yourself, why is he so keen on avoiding a trial," Janan added.

"It is most straightforward," Nissanke asserted. "A prolonged public trial would be an ordeal for all the Tahaku tribe; it's no more than that."

"To that point, my client would like to avoid a trial," Sisay told them.

"And a jury verdict," Ojo said. "Your client is facing the death penalty."

"She would like to avoid that, too."

"What do you have in mind?"

"Mrs. Alemu is willing to accept a manslaughter charge—her husband was abusive, he threatened her violence, and she snapped."

"There is no history in the marriage; no mention of violence o others, no hospital reports…"

"She was too embarrassed to speak of the abuse to others," Sisay claimed. "Even in so close a community as the Tahaku, there are always family secrets."

"And why were there no hospital reports?"

"She was treated by their tribal healer."

"He's the supposed abuser!" Janan yipped.

"He was always very contrite," Kaji told them. "and he never hurt me very badly."

"Less work for him afterward," Janan mumbled.

"He never hurt you badly," Ojo recapped, "and yet you stabbed him to death?"

"My client overreacted," Sisay said.

"It was a hot day, and she is someone much abused over the years," Nissanke explained.

"It sounds to me, a reasonable explanation."

"Did we mention that your client is facing the death penalty?"

"You did—he did, Ms. Takelo…but your evidence is circumstantial."

"Our office finds it persuasive; the grand jury found it compelling enough for an indictment."

"You have no witnesses, a paucity of evidence and a motive that is both contradictory and confusing."

"Most murder convictions are secured without eyewitness testimony," Janan countered, "and there is nothing contradictory in her motive—her spouse was a louse!"

"And his rival, the tribal chief," Ojo capped.

"Your office looks for things to prosecute," Nissanke said, "like hyena out to find a meal."

"Your simile is not very apt," Ojo mentioned. "Unfortunately, we have more than enough cases to keep ourselves busy."

"Then you, too, would prefer avoiding a lengthy and costly trial," Sisay suggested.

"Our preference would be that no murder occurred at all," he told her. "We start every day hoping we'll go out of business."

"My client maintains she was justified, however, she does not want to take any chances; so, we are prepared to accept manslaughter, ten years—you cannot prove intent."

"Manslaughter would be an insult to Mr. Alemu's memory."

"You never met him, that's not such a bad thing," Mrs. Alemu said.

"Murder in the First; three stab wounds, two fatal—life in prison," Ojo countered. "No death penalty."

"But he was cheating on me," Kaji said.

"You were cheating on him," Janan replied.

"He cheated first," Kaji said, sounding like a ten-year-old.

"I might sympathize more, if you weren't willing to frame an innocent man," Ojo told her.

"We can offer you 30 years, a chance at parole in 20—no better than that."

"I'll be sixty-nine," Kaji moaned.

"If this goes to trial, and the jury sees the innocent young man you were willing to sacrifice, they might vote you the death penalty."

Sisay and Kaji conferred a moment, then Sisay asked, "What about 25 years, possible parole in 15?"

After a pause Ojo said, "25; but, parole stays at 20—she ended one life, and threatened to ruin another; she wins no sympathy from us, and I doubt she'll win any from a clear-eyed Ethiopian jury."

"There is no evidence of abuse, only her word," Janan reminded them. "What there is clear evidence of is malice, and callous disregard."

Then Nissanke spoke. "Might there be discretion in where Kaji would serve her sentence? Could she be incarcerated in a facility nearer to the Tahaku lands?"

"We can certainly make that recommendation, but that decision is ultimately up to the Ministry of Justice."

"Will you make that recommendation," Sisay requested.

Ojo nodded. "We will."

Once more, she conferred with her client.

"We agree on the 25…forward us the necessary papers."

"You'll have them by day's end," Janan said.

"I wish a minute or two to speak privately with Kaji," Chief Nissanke told them. "Might we be permitted this?"

It was surprising just to hear Chief Nissanke make a request, not issue an order. "Certainly—just let the guard know when you wish to depart."

As they passed through jail security protocols, Sisay spoke of her client. "She told me she didn't intend to kill him, and I believe her," she told the prosecutors. "Something he said or did triggered years of pent-up anger, or resentment, and coupled with the terrible heat that day…I don't say she's a victim in this, but this killing was not planned."

"Perhaps not planned; but, murderous rage doesn't suddenly bubble up. She may have snapped, Abeda, but she first must have been wound tight enough. Most domestic killings stem from a myriad of provocations, there's nothing alleviative in that."

Ojo didn't speak, but cast his eyes downward; Janan finally stepped in, a bit awkwardly. "Revenge is not the same as anger, and Mrs. Alemu stood to benefit from her husband's death; however you see it, she has to take responsibility."

"But under such circumstances, how can any of us know what we would have done?"

"At some point she picked up a knife," Ojo said, quietly. "It was at that point that any of us are free to make a choice—*that* was when the crime began; her subsequent actions and her lies only serve to compound her guilt. Ms. Sisay, I believe your client knew very well what she was doing the entire time."

Ojo and Janan returned to Zenawi's office, and announced the closing of the case. "Well done, both of you," Zenawi said. "You should also be pleased to know that Otah Ngbato will be released from custody this afternoon, and is already talking to the press about suing for unlawful detention."

"He was a legitimate suspect," Janan dismissed. "The court will dismiss out-of-hand."

"He may get an apology if Adeba Sisay represents him; still, congratulations are in order."

"Sisay was right that our case was circumstantial," Ojo commented, accepting a glass of water. "She might have prevailed, if Kaji Alemu wasn't so afraid of the death penalty."

"It's still barbaric," Janan said. "It's Old Testament—if killing is wrong, it is wrong, period. Many European countries have banned the death penalty."

"And statistically, the effect has been nil—the death penalty remains an effective prosecutorial tool."

"That doesn't make it moral," she argued.

"What would you suggest in its place," Zenawi asked. "If the death penalty is no deterrent to capital crime, if prisons are ineffective in rehabilitation, what is the remedy for society? We cannot eradicate evil—and by the way, just because something is 'Old Testament', doesn't necessarily make it wrong."

"So, Uba, are you flogging your slave for milking your goats on the wrong day?"

He sipped his Scotch. "I'll never tell."

Ojo escorted Janan to her office, and thanked her. "You've done good work in this case, and not all of it easy—you should be proud of yourself."

"Oh, I am!" She smiled, but only briefly, then closed her door. "How are you feeling, Ojo—the matter we discussed the other day..."

He sat. "I spoke with Afia; and as the saying goes, the cards are on the table."

Janan looked concerned. "What are you going to do? Are you thinking of resigning?"

"I don't see how that would change things," he told her. "The decision must be not only an ethical one, but a moral one, as well; and, there's no resigning from that."

"But if you're right, you're living with a killer—and don't just say 'we're all killers'. She may have murdered her own father."

Ojo looked at her sadly. "She may have."

"How can you accept that?"

"I don't know, Janan." He touched her outstretched fingers. "I honestly do not know."

Fourteen.

Near the end of July the Addis Ageur Theatre staged a production of Shakespeare's *A Midsummer Night's Dream*—of course, what other play would have been chosen?—and Ojo and Afia attended, lucky in their mid-auditorium seating, only five rows from the stage. The play was adapted for an East African audience, of course; but with the *Dream* that scarcely mattered, as it could be set on Mars as readily as ancient Athens.

And on the drive home Afia said as much.

"So what was Shakespeare saying," she asked, as she tapped her long fingers on the steering-wheel.

"that life is a dream is an old Renaissance trope, it goes perhaps back to ancient Greece, to Aeschylus, on to the 'Row Your Boat' song...is Shakespeare saying we shape and form our own reality?"

"Maybe that reality is relative," Ojo offered.

"That same world is so different for Theseus than Oberon, for Helena than Puck, or the mechanicals—like that story about describing the elephant, as it were." Ojo of course actually used the names used in the Amharic version.

"Of course, everyone makes that comparison."

"And that business with the love potion she continued. "What juice from a Western flower does that? Who was he kidding?"

"It's just a device," Ojo dismissed. "And, who knows—maybe such a flower grew near ancient Athens, and it has died out by now; after all, Sappho refers to love potions."

"How would Shakespeare know that? He knew Ovid, and Ovid's Sappho never mentions love potions in the *Heroides*."

"That's what bothers you," he kidded. "not girding the earth in ninety seconds, not the ass's ears; but, the love potion...?"

"It was the one unbelievable part." Afia tried but failed to keep a straight face.

They came home late, as even adapted Shakespeare plays are long affairs, and Afia asked if she should open their last bottle of wine. "I won't have a glass, but please go ahead if you want one."

She was halfway to opening the bottle, when she paused. "I have been drinking more," she said aloud, but possibly more to herself. "I have been—and, not because it's summer."

"But for that reason, too," Ojo quietly remarked. "It's been a very hard time for us."

"But I should not be seeking an excuse, and yes, reasons are different. I should be stronger than this; I would like to be stronger."

"There is a chemical component."

No; not yet," she asserted. "It was a choice to start drinking more, and so is a choice to drink less, even during an immoderate summer."

"Besides, alcohol is a dehydrating agent—it's not a liquid that aids in hydration."

"Like mercury?" Afia smiled.

Ojo had to agree. "If you drink mercury, you no longer need to worry about hydrating!"

"Do you know, it's been an entire month almost, since I've visited an online gambling site?

I have not given in, not once…" She opened the wine bottle, and poured a glass. "And, I've joined a Gambling Anonymous support group; my first virtual meeting is next week. And since we meet remotely, you can oversee my progress."

"That is all good," Ojo said.

She sat beside him, and spoke lowly. "I thought myself stronger than I was—I thought I could control its influence, unlike all the others who inevitably fall victim…of course, I thought *I* was the exception. Evil is like that."

"Evil?"

"I know what I've done," Afia said, then touched her flat stomach. "but I wouldn't let you worry unnecessarily for one moment." What did she mean, what did her gesture mean—that as long as she was safe, as long as her child is safe, he will be safe—until he develops a heart condition?

"If it becomes necessary,—" he started, but Afia cut him off, quickly upset, then quickly once more in control.

"You misunderstand me, even now—Ojo, even if were to tell you everything, you could never know whether I was lying; even if I were to confess while talking in my sleep, I would be asleep—you would have heard words from a dream."

He glanced to her wine glass. "How long will that help you?"

"Perhaps, you're right," she said; she then poured the wine in her glass down the sink in the kitchen, and returned with water instead. "I won't have this conversation again, Ojo; you are not married to *La Belle Dame*...I love you, and soon we will be a family."

He glanced to her narrow waist, a bit pinched in her evening dress. "I've been considering leaving the Prosecutor's Office," he told her.

"What? Why?"

He looked at her a moment. Of course, she was the reason, she was certainly the only reason. But if he said so, he was admitting that not opposing her was tantamount to breaking his professional oath, even when both knew it was.

"It's a question of ethics," he simply said.

"You have read the Conan Doyle stories; 'The Devil's Foot', 'The Abbey Grange'—do you disagree with Sherlock Holmes?" In both stories to which she alluded, killers were let go free.

"It's a false analogy; besides, Sherlock Holmes never existed."

"You shouldn't resign, you are a fine prosecutor; and what you might feel just now, will pass...and, didn't you just successfully close your first capital case?"

"It never went to trial," Ojo said.

Afia smiled. "Some lawyers go to court only a handful of times in their careers—some never face a jury; I read that, so it must be true."

He took the glass from her gently, sipped, and looked into her lovely eyes. "Did you sneak in some of that love potion from Puck?" Puck—who never existed, either.

"You could search me for that tiny western flower," she cooed, and wigged herself closer.

He unclasped the dress in the back, but paused at the zipper. "Is this where we are—is this us from now on?"

She set down her empty glass. "It looks like it."

"We just accept it." He didn't know what response to expect, or what he wanted to hear; certainly not a confession, which would never come.

Afia glanced to the window, and the darkness beyond. "Ojo, there are over 80 million Ethiopians out there, most of whom will not have enough food to get through tomorrow—most of them. We have been *so* lucky, perhaps luckier than we had any right to be—if we cannot make peace with the world we're in, we can at least make our peace with ourselves, and each other."

Ojo stared at her. "And, the law...?"

"Man's law, or God's, as delivered by men thousands of years ago?" She stood from the couch, and started upstairs. "In this world of predator and prey, what is the law?"

Perhaps it was a spurious argument, but Ojo made no response as she vanished up the stairs. He sat lost in thought as he heard her in the washroom, then thought he heard her enter the bedroom—he most likely didn't, as Afia was light on her feet.

Some time later he went upstairs himself, and on entering the bedroom found Afia already asleep. She slept naked, as he imagined did most Ethiopians—she was naked, asleep, vulnerable, and Ojo knew that when he climbed in beside her, as she also slept lightly, he would rouse her.

His suspicions could never be proved, and in the end all he had was what he believed had happened; that's all he ever had, he thought—belief in God, belief in the future, and in a system that was flawed, antiquated, limited...and still he believed in Afia and in their life together, now knit by monstrous decisions they'd made—hers, and now his.

www.ingramcontent.com/pod-product-compliance
Lightning Source LLC
LaVergne TN
LVHW090045160826
845672LV00015B/1566

* 9 7 9 8 8 4 7 4 1 5 2 0 0 *